Angel Kisses

An Instalove Military Romance

Nichole Rose

CONTENTS

Dedication

To 2022. Don't make us riot.

About the Book

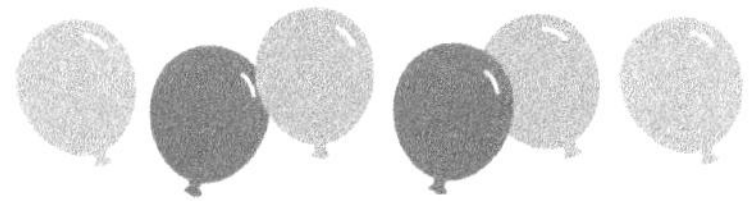

A little New Years' magic will send a former SEAL and his curvy girl up in flames.

Masen Starks

Six months ago, I found my future.

Theia Perry is the sweetest little angel I've ever met.

When I'm with her, I'm invincible.

But she doesn't need a damaged soldier like me messing up her life.

I shouldn't have asked her to this New Year's Eve party.

But I can't bring myself to regret it.

She deserves better than me.

But before the clock strikes midnight, she'll be mine in every way.

Theia Perry

When I took a job working with veterans, I never thought I'd fall for one.

Masen Starks is a legitimate hero.

And the man of my dreams.

To him, I'm just a curvy college kid and orphaned Army brat.

But when he asks me to the annual New Year's Eve party, I jump at the chance.

One way or another, I'm going to prove that I'm more than he sees.

Tonight, I'm going to be the woman he can't resist.

When this younger curvy girl decides to go get her older SEAL, she ignites more than just fireworks. If you enjoy steamy holiday romance, bossy SEALs, and sassy heroines, you'll love Masen and Theia's sugary-sweet and extra steamy story!

Chapter One
Theia

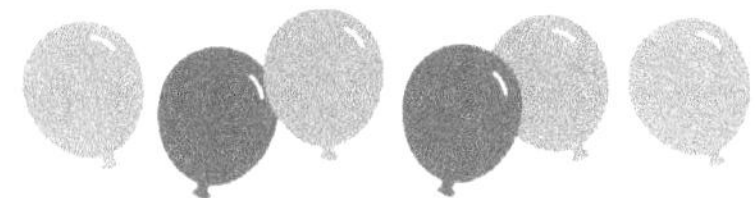

<u>**S**ix Months Ago</u>

"Holy crap," I whisper, coming to a dead stop in the middle of the hallway. Liberty Thorne crashes into me from behind, knocking me forward two steps. I thrust my hand out toward the wall, grasping onto the cool tiles to keep myself upright.

"I'm so sorry," Liberty says, grasping my arm to help steady me.

"It was my fault," I mumble, my cheeks blazing with heat. It's my first day here, and she's married to my new boss. I don't want her thinking I'm a hopeless klutz even though I generally am. But this time, I have an excuse. A six-foot, shirtless excuse.

My gaze darts back to the man who caught my attention.

He looks like a wild animal stalking toward us, rivulets of sweat dripping down his broad chest. His dark hair is plastered to his forehead with two small chunks of it standing upright as if in a mohawk. He hasn't spotted us. He's too focused on the hunk of metal in his hands...both of which are covered in grease. Spots of it adorn his golden skin too, turning them a sickly green color. A nasty scar runs down his right side, as if someone took a knife and split him open from his ribcage to his hip. It's still new enough to be red and puckered.

I don't have to guess to know he's military. I've spent enough time around soldiers to recognize them when I see them. I'm an Army brat. My dad was enlisted until the day he died. I grew up on base under the watchful eyes of the men he commanded.

Like my dad and his unit, most of the men here have been to hell and back. They're Special Forces, Rangers, SEALs...the men who saw things no one should ever have to see on missions they can't even discuss. Whoever this man is, he's spent time in the trenches too. I don't even need the SEAL tattoos on his arms and chest to know this. His scar, the darkness clinging to him, and the way he moves tells the story.

He's graceful, quiet on his feet even though he shouldn't be. At his size, his steps should thunder down the hall. They don't. He doesn't make a sound as he strides toward us, his long legs quickly covering the distance. He's dangerous. But he's beautiful too. Like a storm.

"Hey, Mase," Liberty says, lifting her hand in a wave.

His head shoots upward, two blue eyes pinning me in place. As soon as his gaze lands on me, all the air in my lungs escapes with a whoosh. There are so many shades of blue in his eyes, it's unreal. They're like ice toward the pupil, gradually darkening toward the outer rim. The stark hopelessness in them cracks my heart in half.

He freezes in mid-step, his nostrils flaring as if he's scenting prey.

For a long moment, we just stare at each other.

The sorrow in his gaze burns through me, making me ache in places I didn't know I could ache for someone else. Whatever he's been through, whatever brought him to Killian's program...it wasn't good. My heart cries out in protest, aching to soothe him. It's not just the searing grief in his eyes that elicits that response, either. It's a feeling more than anything, a little voice demanding I help him.

It's quiet, little more than a whisper, but my body actually twitches with the urge to move closer to him.

Energy hums between us as I stare at him, caught between the urge to hug him and the realization that I don't even know him. His eyes heat and darken as he stares back. The desire blazing to life in them raises the fine hairs on my arms, turning my skin to gooseflesh. Answering desire stirs deep in my womb, touching me as powerfully as the urge to hug him.

A soft growl rumbles in his throat as if he knows what I'm thinking.

The dark sound vibrates my bones.

My nipples are hard points in my thin blouse. I cross my arms over my chest, trying to hide the way he affects me. His gaze drops from my face to my chest, making a slow crawl down my body. The interest in his eyes is obvious. Mine probably matches.

My father's ghost growls a *hell no* from the grave.

He only ever had one rule for me. Not to get involved with a man like him.

This man makes me want to break that rule. Defiance bubbles up from my stomach, threatening to send me right into his arms. Odd, considering that I've never been in any man's arms. Never wanted to be before now. I barely understand the intense ache, but I know instinctively that feeling this stranger's strong arms close around me will be the only thing to take it away again.

"Theia, this is Masen Starks," Liberty says, startling me. I forgot she was here. "He's working through the End of Service program. He does a lot of work to help us out. Masen, this is Theia Perry. She'll be running the daycare a few days a week."

"Theia Perry," Masen says, almost as if he's testing my name on his full lips. It certainly sounds better coming from his than it does mine. His deep voice hums like a purr, touching places inside me that send a shiver of delight through my system.

"Hi, Masen," I say. His name shakes on my lips. I inhale a deep breath and paste a smile on my face, trying not to let him see how much he's affected me. I think he knows though.

His lips tip up into a small grin, turning him from fierce, broken warrior to wicked little boy. The grief in his eyes fades, making them lighter.

"You just finished your final assignment?" I ask.

"In Sudan," he says. Pain flashes in his eyes before he quickly masks it.

My heart aches at the sight of it.

"My dad spent some time over there," I say softly. Even if I asked what he saw over there, he couldn't tell me. The veterans served here are all returning from highly classified missions. Killian's organization is the only one in the United States that serves men like Masen. "He used to tell me stories about the pyramids."

"Your dad was military?"

"Army Special Forces." I give him a small smile, resisting the urge to fidget beneath the weight of his stare. It's intense, like every bit of attention he possesses is focused solely on me. "Um, I'm glad you made it home safely."

I bite my tongue before I can blurt out a thanks for his service. My dad always told me that nothing annoys veterans more than being thanked for something most people don't fully understand. It's especially unhelpful when they're fighting just to make it through the day.

"You work with kids, Theia?"

"Yes."

His grin widens. The darkness in his eyes fades a little more.

"I'm good with them," I supply, though I'm not sure why.

"I bet they love you."

"Maybe."

He takes a step toward me.

"Do you like kids?" I blurt the question like a crazy person, practically shouting it into the silence.

For some reason, the question makes him flinch. His expression twists and darkens, like the question sucked a little of the light out of them, but I don't know why.

"Never spent much time around them," he mutters.

"Liar," Liberty says with a quiet laugh. "My boys love him."

She and her husband, Killian, have two boys. They both attend the daycare here. I can't wait to meet them. I can't wait to meet the other kids either and help their parents reacclimate to parenthood. That's my real job here, helping soldiers like Masen make the transition from whatever classified missions they've been on to parenthood.

"Your boys are too young to know better," Masen says, his voice somber. "Men like me have no business around kids. I'd probably scar them for life."

"That's not true," I say, my voice soft. "My dad didn't scar me for life."

"He's retired now?"

"He died on his last mission," I whisper. My heart throbs at the reminder. Even though it's been five years, it still hurts. I miss him every day.

"Shit," Masen says, regret searing his expression. "I'm sorry, baby girl."

"Me too."

"You still have your mom?"

Liberty fidgets beside me.

"No. He was my only family."

"Fuck."

My eyes widen when Masen curses.

"How old are you, Theia?"

"Twenty-two."

He takes a step away from me, glancing from me to Liberty. "You need to keep an eye on her," he growls to her. "She's too goddamn young to be around half these men."

I blanche at his comment, my eyes widening. Indignation runs through me, my heart thumping hard against my ribcage. Embarrassment follows hot on its heels. The last thing I need is for Liberty and Killian to start thinking I'm too young for this job. I may only be twenty-two, but I know what I'm doing. I'm working on my graduate degree in clinical psychology. And I've been volunteering with veterans for a long time.

"I'm more than capable of looking out for myself," I snap to Masen. "I've been doing it for half my life."

He opens his mouth to argue, but Liberty cuts him off.

"She'll be fine," she says, her voice firm. "She's been working with veterans and their families for years now. We're excited to have her here."

Masen growls a curse, shaking his head. His icy eyes meet mine again.

I tip my chin up, silently daring him to say whatever he's thinking.

Instead, he mutters another curse beneath his breath and then shakes his head. "Guess that's settled then," he says. "I'll be seeing you around, Theia."

The way he says it almost makes it sound like a threat.

Even though I shouldn't like it...I do.

"Oh, hey," I say, glancing up from my desk as Masen steps into the daycare. As usual, his hands are stained black with grease. Spots of it dot his Navy t-shirt too. The fabric clings to his body in a way that's far too appealing. Everything about him is appealing to me. Unfortunately, I don't think he feels the same.

He stops in almost every day the daycare is open to check on me, but he always keeps a polite distance between us. He's changed a lot since I started here three months ago. He seems less haunted now. I hope that's because he's finally found a little peace. Part of me hopes I had something to do with it even though I don't see how that's possible.

He never says much when he stops by. Honestly, I think he only checks in because he thinks I need a babysitter. I gave up months ago reminding him that I know how to take care of myself. He never listens. He just grunts and then comes back again the next day to check on me.

It drives me crazy! He looks at me sometimes like he wants nothing more than to pull me into his arms, but he never follows through. Honestly, he usually finds a reason to run off again moments later, like he doesn't trust himself to be around me or something.

The kids love him. His burden seems a little lighter when he's around them. I'm still not sure what he saw in Sudan, but I've learned enough about him to be able to put a few pieces together. Whatever happened over there involved children. Child soldiers, maybe.

Whatever it was, the kids here help, so I don't ask him not to come. I don't think I could even if I wanted to. The more time I spend around him, the harder it is to get him out of my head. It's been months, and I spend most of every day thinking about him, waiting for him to appear in the doorway. A big part of me dreads the day he doesn't appear. He'll be finished with the program soon. It's going to break my heart when he leaves.

"It's storming," he says, letting the glass door swing closed behind him.

"I noticed." I cut my eyes toward the row of windows across the room and then look back at him. Rain falls in sheets outside. The sky is dark, and periodic claps of thunder rattle the windows in their frames.

Masen narrows his eyes on me like he knows I'm teasing him. I can't help it though. He's so rigid all the time! It makes me want to ruffle him just a little bit. I've never felt that way about anyone before. But this one... Lord, the things this one makes me want.

"I've been trying to wait it out," I say when he takes a step toward my desk.

"Good idea." He stops walking toward me and scans the small room.

I follow his gaze to the artwork the kids did this morning. Most of it is little more than scribbles across bright pieces of construction paper, but they were so excited to hang it on the walls. I know the second Masen notices the picture Liberty's oldest, Spencer, drew. The kid is going to be an amazing artist one day.

"What's this?" Masen asks, pointing at it.

"I believe that's you and Killian," I say, my voice soft. "Spencer drew it."

Masen turns those blue eyes on me, silently asking for an explanation.

"They were drawing pictures of heroes." Most of the kids drew superheroes, or scribbles that represented superheroes. Not Spencer. He drew Masen and his dad. He even gave them the scars they carry—Masen's across his side and Killian's across his cheek.

"He thinks I'm a hero?"

"Most people do," I say.

He grunts instead of responding.

I start packing up my desk. After three months, I'm used to his silence. It's...peaceful in a way. Calming. I like being around him far more than I probably should.

"I'm done with the program."

My heart drops into my feet. I bump the stack of paperwork on the side of my desk, knocking half of it onto the floor. For a minute, the world just...stops spinning. And then it lurches into motion again with a sickening thud.

Masen closes the distance between us and crouches to pick up the sheets of paper now scattered around my desk. I sit completely still, trying to process the fact that he's leaving. I'm not sure where to even begin though. I've known it was coming for weeks now. But I somehow wasn't prepared for the reality.

Tears fill my eyes. I quickly blink them back before Masen sees them.

When he rises to his feet, his eyes lock on my face and I know my attempt was useless. He sees them. He sets the papers down on the desk, reaching one hand out toward me. Right before he touches my cheek, he pulls back.

"You're sad," he says. It's not a question but I feel compelled to explain anyway. I feel guilty for being sad when finishing the program means he's doing better. He's made enough progress to be ready to face the world on his own. That's a good thing. And yet...and yet it doesn't *feel* like a good thing to me.

"I'm happy for you," I say, clearing my throat. "I just got used to seeing you around here. That's all." I avoid his gaze and busy myself with the paperwork, restacking it neatly. I feel him watching me though. I always feel the weight of his gaze on me.

"Theia."

I reluctantly meet his gaze.

"I'm not someone worth missing, baby girl."

He means it. But he's wrong.

I shove the rest of my stuff into my purse with shaking hands. Part of me wants to wrap them around his broad shoulders and shake sense into him. The other part knows it wouldn't do any good. He's stubborn and unyielding. Once he's made up his mind, there is no changing it.

"You're mad."

"I'm not," I lie, trying to slide around him.

He doesn't let me go. He cages me in between my desk and the bulletin board behind me, the heat of his body searing into me. He's standing closer than he ever has before. I smell his cologne and the sweat on his skin. I see the follicles on his scruffy jaw.

My stomach dips and spins, desire shooting through me like a bolt. I have to lock my legs in place to keep from leaning into his hard chest.

"You don't want me to go," he says, tipping my chin up until I meet his gaze.

"I...didn't say that."

He narrows his eyes on me.

"I'm allowed to miss whoever I want to miss."

His lips twitch. "You're mad at me for not wanting you to miss me?"

"No." I roll my eyes, and then push against his ridiculously hard chest. "I'm not mad at you. I'm annoyed with you and I'm sad for you."

"Why?"

"It doesn't matter. Let me go."

"Tell me why."

"No."

"Theia."

I growl in frustration. Why do men think they can say our names in that tone, and we'll obey? And why does it make me want to obey him? He's so frustrating!

"It doesn't matter, Masen."

"It matters, sunflower."

"I'm not sure which hurts more," I say, giving in. Every time he calls me *sunflower*, I melt. "The fact that you believe you aren't worth missing...or the fact that you want me to believe it so badly." I push against his chest again, breathing a sigh of relief when he stumbles back a step, allowing me to dart around him.

When I look back at the door, he's still standing in the same spot, his hands clenched into fists, his eyes on the floor.

"Bye, Masen," I whisper, slipping out of the room with tears in my eyes and a hole in my heart.

He might not want me to miss him, but I don't think I'll ever stop.

CHAPTER TWO
Masen

Present

"The freezer is growling at me again."

I glance up from my desk to find Liberty Thorne standing in the doorway of my office, her hands on her wide hips. Strands of her dark hair have fallen from the bun on top of her head to frame her round face. Her irritated expression makes me smile.

Liberty is one of those women men fight wars over. Most of the men here would certainly fight to the death to protect her, and not because her husband, Killian, would expect nothing less. The men here genuinely respect her. I know I do.

I can count on one hand the number of people I consider friends. She's at the top of the list. When I arrived here a little over six months ago, I had no plans, no place to go. Nothing but an ugly scar across my side and a whole lot of free time.

I've been on my own my entire life, bouncing from foster home to foster home. Like most kids in the same boat, I joined up as soon as I turned eighteen.

I always thought I'd be in until I died. And then my team was sent to Sudan.

Eight of us went in to rescue a group of children from the TPLF. Only three of us made it out alive. You expect to lose people in the middle of a warzone. You don't expect it to be children. That fucked me up worse than finding myself at the business end of a militia member's dagger.

I didn't re-up. When my contract expired, my former Commander sent me here, said I needed this place even if I was too goddamn stubborn to admit it. He wasn't wrong.

Killian's program is designed for motherfuckers like me. Those who go to war and come back a little fucked up over things they can't discuss. Being haunted is a hell of a thing when you can't even tell the world what haunts you, what hurts you. It's different here. Every man here carries the same burden, sees the same sort of things when they close their eyes.

I finally sleep at night because of this place and what I learned here.

I finished the program months ago but I'm still here. Killian would have kicked my ass to the curb long ago, but Liberty convinced him to give me an office instead. Whatever needs doing, I do. Working with my hands is peaceful, soothing. It's a handy skill to have in a place this size. Something is always breaking, broken, or fucked up beyond repair.

That's not the reason I'm still here.

The promise of peace drew me to this place. Theia Perry keeps me here.

She's the sweetest little angel I've ever met in my life. Her big blue eyes knocked me on my ass the first time I saw her. For months before meeting her, all I saw was blood and death. Grief and pain burned me alive, every minute of the fucking day. Her blue eyes cut right through both, hacking away at it like they were determined to get to the man beneath.

She brought me back to life, gave me the push I needed to crawl out of the pit I was in. She nearly cried when I told her I finished the program. I knew right then and there that I wouldn't be leaving. I couldn't. I've spent the months since working my ass off to become someone who might one day stand a chance in hell of deserving a woman like her.

I'm closer than I've ever been...and yet still not close enough.

I want to make her mine more than I want my next breath. Unfortunately for me, Theia is light years out of my league. She's sunshine and rainbows. And I'm...not. The program here might have saved my life, but it didn't fix me. When you live in the dark for so long, eventually you become a part of it. The shadow rubs off on you, soils you.

I'm dirty beyond repair. My hands are stained in blood and worse.

And she's too goddamn pure to soil. But fuck, how I want to stain her anyway.

I spend at least half of each day trying to imagine exactly what her curves would feel like beneath my rough hands, or how loud she'd purr if I wrapped her blonde hair up in my fist while taking her from behind.

She has no fucking clue that I'm building a house for her. She doesn't know a lot of things, truth be told. I think she's still pissed at me for telling her I wasn't a man worth missing. I don't know. But she tries like hell to ignore me. I never let her get away with it, but it doesn't stop her from trying. She's a stubborn little thing.

"Have you tried growling back?" I ask Liberty.

"You're not nearly as funny as you think you are," she retorts, narrowing her eyes on me. She can't fool me though. I see her lips twitching.

"I'm fucking hilarious, and you know it," I say, deadpan.

"You're a legend in your own mind, Masen Starks."

"No comment."

She cracks a smile.

"I already ordered the part for the freezer." I fish through the riot of paperwork on my desk for the purchase order. I find it stuck to a stack of maintenance requests with what I'm pretty sure is ketchup. I'm also pretty sure it didn't come from me. I hate ketchup. "What the fuck?"

Liberty laughs when I hold it up. "You need a secretary."

"The last thing I need is a secretary," I mutter, tossing the stack of papers down in disgust. "What I need is a blowtorch." Paperwork is not my strong suit. I fucking loathe it. Unfortunately, this job seems to come with a helluva lot of it, especially since Killian hired a carpenter and a handyman to help me out around here. I somehow went from being the hired help to being the boss of the hired help, and I'm still not entirely sure how that happened.

"It could be worse," Liberty says, crossing her arms and leaning up against the doorjamb. She rarely actually comes into my office. Killian is a possessive bastard. For months, he looked at me sideways anytime I even spoke to her. He trusts no one with his wife, especially now that she's pregnant. "You could be the one who has to sign checks for everything."

I grunt in response, glad that shit isn't part of my job. "The part will be in sometime after the New Year. The freezer will be fine until then. It's a faulty evaporator fan."

"I'll let Killian know."

"Is he still in the south wing?"

Liberty nods.

"I'll let him know. I need to go over there anyway."

"To see Theia?"

"To take measurements," I say. We're planning to build a playground for the kids right outside of the daycare. It'll be a pain in the ass, but Theia suggested it, and I'm damn sure not going to tell her no. Neither is Killian. She's good with the kids. Hell, she's good with everyone. There's something calming about her, something peaceful.

I'm not the only one who feels it. I spend half my goddamn time running men off from around her. They flock like bees to her sweetness. She's oblivious to it, naturally. She just thinks spending time around the kids settles them. I see the way they look at her though. If they thought they stood a chance, they'd be beating down her fucking door to get to her.

Most of them know not to even try getting close to her. They learn that lesson quick when they get here. I make sure of it. If anyone even thinks about putting a hand on her, they'll answer to me. She deserves better than a former SEAL with no family and no home. But she's mine anyway. Or she will be soon.

"And see Theia," Liberty says, grinning at me.

I shrug instead of denying it. Liberty figured out why I'm still here months ago.

"You should ask her to the New Year's Eve party, Mase," she says, her voice soft. How she talked Killian into throwing a party, I don't know. The man doesn't know the definition of party. But he agreed to make his wife happy. They're going all out for everyone in the program. Even hired a decorator to turn the rec hall into a ballroom. Fireworks are a problem for a lot of us, so he hired a band too, something to drown out the sounds that drag us back to places we don't want to go.

"Didn't plan on going," I mutter.

"Eventually, she's going to say yes to someone," Liberty says.

I scowl at her.

"Don't look at me like that," she says, unperturbed. "You know it's true. The guys ask her out all the time, and she turns them down. But she won't wait forever, Mase. Eventually, she's going to say yes to someone. We both know she wants that person to be you."

"She shouldn't," I growl. It's the truth. I'm the last person she should want.

"Why not? You're in love with her."

"I'm going to see Killian," I say, rising to my feet. I'm not interested in having this conversation, especially not with Liberty. She may have grown up in foster care like I did, but she doesn't know darkness. Killian makes damn sure it doesn't touch her life. If she knew the things I want to do to Theia, she wouldn't be here now, suggesting I ask her out.

I don't want her soft and sweet like she deserves. I want to tie her to my bed and fuck her until she breaks. I want my handprints on her ass while she's choking on my length. She's a virgin, innocence dripping from her. And I want to possess every single one of her holes with one hand around her throat and my name on her lips. I want to be her first and only. So goddamn badly it's torture. But I have nothing to offer her beyond eight inches and PTSD. She deserves more. Hell, she deserves everything.

Patience is a virtue, but I'm running out of it.

"Fine. But don't say I didn't warn you," Liberty says and then shakes her head and walks away.

"Fuck," I growl, clenching my fists. The last fucking thing I want to think about right now is Theia going to this party with someone else. Theia, smiling at someone else. Theia, falling in love with someone else.

She's mine, goddammit.

Except how the fuck is a guy like me supposed to be worthy of an angel?

"You coming to the party this weekend?" Killian asks, eyeing me levelly.

"Didn't plan on it. Hold this." I hand him the end of the tape measure and then move to the corner of the building, carefully measuring the length of the courtyard. The shrill wind hits the tape, sending the yellow length twisting and turning back and forth.

I grip it more firmly and press it to the side of the building, trying to ensure the measurement is correct. I check it twice and then call it out to Killian.

"It'll be tight," he says, striding toward me.

"We can make it work."

He jerks his chin in a nod. Killian doesn't say much. He's a hard ass, only soft when it comes to his wife, kids, and little sisters. He has no problem hurting your feelings, *especially* when it comes to them. It took him fucking forever to realize I'm not trying to poach his wife from him. Couldn't even if I tried...which I wouldn't do. She's a friend, nothing more. And Killian is the only man she sees. They've been married for five years and are still very much in love.

I respect the hell out of her and Killian. They care about the people here and what happens to them. Most people talk about the good deeds they'd do if they could afford it. Killian isn't one who talks. He acts. His own trust fund keeps this place running, and I know damn well it isn't cheap. He never balks or bats a lash though. This place is the best thing that will ever happen to most of the men here. When they leave for civilian life, it'll be with a clear head and a fresh start.

"Heard Theia is going," Killian says.

"Jesus fucking Christ," I mutter, shaking my head. I should have known Liberty talked him into bringing this up. I ignore him and start the next measurement.

"Heard Marco Alvarez plans to ask her to go as his date."

I will tie bricks to Marco's feet and drown him in the ocean. Won't even feel badly about doing it. I don't tell

Killian that though. I just grunt, hoping he takes the hint. He doesn't.

"You going to get your head out of your ass and claim her sometime soon?" he demands.

"No disrespect intended, but that's my business."

"I'm making it mine."

"Did Liberty put you up to this?" I growl.

"Nope." He jerks his chin toward the building. Theia is on the other side of those windows, reading to the kids. I don't even have to look to know that's what she's doing right now. I memorized her schedule months ago. I can time it down to the minute. "But my wife considers Theia family, which means Theia is my family too. Her daddy isn't here to tell you to get your head out of your ass, so I'm doing the honors."

"Noted," I say, hoping to put an end to the conversation. All goddamn day, I've been thinking about what Liberty said this morning, about Theia saying yes to someone else. It's pissing me off. The men here have been on the receiving end of every type of honor the military has to offer. And I'd feel zero remorse for killing any of them for touching her.

If I don't deserve her, they damn sure don't. Especially not fucking Marco Alvarez. He's fucked his way through every continent he's stepped foot on. He doesn't know the first thing about loving a woman like Theia.

I doubt he could even tell you the first thing about her beyond the fact that she's beautiful and sweet and her laughter sounds like music. He doesn't know that she misses her dad intensely or that she gets shy as hell when she's nervous. He doesn't know that she cries when she watches Land Before Time with the kids. He doesn't know how strong she is or just how big her heart is. He doesn't know that she almost cried when I told her I wasn't someone worth missing.

He doesn't know that she dances in her kitchen or devours steamy romance books in one sitting. He doesn't know what she looks like with her reading glasses perched on her nose and her hair up in a messy bun. He doesn't know *her*, not like I do.

I've been watching her for six months, finding reasons to visit the daycare every damn day just to see her. Even though she knows I'm going to show up at some point, she still looks surprised every time she sees me. She looks relieved too, even though she tries to hide it. I doubt she'd admit it if I asked. She's stubborn as hell.

Every damn time I see her, she tells me she doesn't need a babysitter, like she thinks that's the only reason I check in on her. Like she has no clue I'm still here because she is.

My innocent little sunflower doesn't have a clue that my dick hangs heavy in my pants all day every day because of her, or that I'm so fucking in love with her it's pathetic. She doesn't know that I've been following her for months, watching every move she makes because I can't stop myself.

"What's the issue?" Killian asks. "You think you aren't good enough? She deserves better?"

"Something like that," I mutter.

"Figured as much."

We work in silence for a minute, getting measurements for the far side of the courtyard. Two different wings of the building intersect on this side, throwing the area into shadow. It's cooler underneath. It's a good place for a metal slide or two. It won't get hot enough to burn the kids.

"You aren't good enough for her," Killian says once we're done.

I lift my head to look at him.

"You aren't," he says with a shrug. The scar bisecting his cheek lends a certain severity to his expression. He's a lethal motherfucker who pulls no punches. "None of us are. We've got blood on our hands and war in our souls. We've done things we can't take back, no matter how much we wish we could."

"What's your point?"

"My point is that it's time for you to get the fuck over it," he says, narrowing his dark eyes on me. "You ever heard of a self-fulfilling prophecy?"

I nod.

"You'll never be good enough for her. Doesn't matter how long or how hard you try; you won't ever feel like you deserve her. But waiting around to make a move isn't doing a damn thing beyond proving you right. The longer you wait, the less you deserve her."

He's not entirely wrong. He's not entirely right either.

"I'm building her a house," I say.

His eyes widen.

"Figure I should at least have some place to take her besides back to my room here." I shove the tape measure into my pocket, shaking my head. "That's the hold up, not any of the other bullshit. I knew months ago that I'd never deserve her. Knew she was mine long before that. Now, I'd appreciate if you'd help me measure this fucking courtyard instead of grilling me about shit that's not your business."

"Fair enough," Killian mutters, holding his hands up in a gesture of surrender.

I breathe a quiet sigh of relief, grateful he's letting the subject go. Not having her in my bed is hard enough already. I don't know how much longer I can wait to make her mine before I snap. My self-control has been on the verge of slipping for months already.

I already know it's not going to take much to tip me over the edge.

Chapter Three
Theia

"Please start," I whisper to my car before turning the key. The engine whirrs like it's trying to turn over, but it doesn't start. I heave a sigh and give up. I need a new battery or starter or whatever it is that makes the car start reliably, but it's after six and I just want to go home and eat my feelings.

I've had a lot of those lately. Holidays are always tough when you're alone. When my dad was alive, he always made a big deal out of Christmas. Now that he's gone, it just doesn't seem as magical as it did before I lost him. Liberty and Killian were kind enough to invite me to celebrate with them. I had a good time but seeing them so blissfully happy just made me feel even more lonely.

I missed Masen like crazy. When he told me he was done with the program three months ago, it broke my heart. I came in for my next shift expecting him to be gone. But he was still here.

Every day I work, I wait with bated breath for him to appear in the doorway of the daycare. Then and only then do I feel like I can breathe easy. And then I repeat the process all over again the next time, terrified he's going to disappear between one shift and the next.

Even though he works for Killian full-time now, I still worry that he'll leave.

I wanted to ask him to spend Christmas with me, but I chickened out. I was afraid he'd say no. I should have asked though. I just ended up spending the entire day regretting the fact that I didn't ask. Worrying that we'd get back to work today, and he'd be gone.

Not knowing why he decided to stay is making me crazy. But I'm not brave enough to ask him that question either. I want it to be because of me so damn badly. But I'm terrified it's not. It's been three months and he hasn't made a move. I think he still sees me as someone he needs to look out for, someone who needs a babysitter. And I don't know how to make him see me differently.

What I know about men, I learned from watching my dad and his team. They cracked jokes and said filthy things, but as soon as they realized I could hear, they'd go silent. My dad would have lost his mind if he knew half the things I heard. But none of it was particularly useful. I know nothing about seducing a man like Masen or making him see me as anything more than a curvy college kid.

I'm determined to figure it out. It might be silly, but my New Year's resolution is to make Masen fall in love with me. I just have to figure out how I'm supposed to make that happen.

As if thinking about him conjured him up, he appears on the far side of the parking lot, looking far too damn beautiful with his dark hair all messed up and his scruffy jaw. His gaze immediately lands on my car. Even from a distance, those icy blue eyes sear into me, pinning me in place.

My heartrate speeds up, heat unfurling in my stomach. The way he looks at me...God, I'd kill to see that look on his face every single day for the rest of my life. There's so much heat in his gaze, so much emotion swirling through his eyes. And I don't understand any of it.

His gaze shifts from mine, his face falling into a dark scowl as he looks at something on the opposite side of the parking lot. I turn my head to see what he's looking at.

"Great," I groan when I see Marco Alvarez coming out of the building. Marco is a former Marine. He's a nice guy, but he annoys me. He's loud and brash and never shuts up. I'm pretty sure he's a manwhore. He's never inappropriate toward me. Just...annoying.

I do not want to deal with him right now. The universe refuses to throw me a bone though. Marco sees me sitting in my car and starts moving in my direction. I groan again and try to crank the engine. It barely even clicks this time.

"Pop the hood, sunflower."

"Ahh!" I scream, practically jumping out of my seat when Masen's voice sounds from the passenger side. I whip my head in his direction to see him standing at the window, his lips compressed into a thin line. "You scared the crap out of me!"

"I noticed." His expression sours further. "You should pay more attention to your surroundings."

"I was busy."

"Staring at Marco."

"More like hoping the ground would open up and swallow him before he made it over here," I mutter, wrinkling my nose at the thought of staring at Marco. "He reminds me of Johnny Bravo."

"The one-man army." Masen's lips twitch, his expression softening.

"Everything okay?" Marco asks, drawing to a stop a few feet from my car.

"I've got it handled," Masen says, his firm tone leaving no room for argument.

Marco glances from him to me. I lift my hand in a wave, pasting a bright smile on my face that I hope he takes as confirmation that he's not needed here. He's not. Definitely not.

"Cool," he says and then turns to jog back across the lot.

I exhale a relieved sigh.

"Pop the hood," Masen says again.

I reach for the hood release and pull it. The hood clicks open, lifting an inch from the frame. Masen moves to the front of the car, lifting it the rest of the way. I undo my seatbelt and climb from the car, pulling my jacket closed around me. Winters in California are mild, but even the desert gets cold when the sun sinks below the horizon.

"I think it's my battery," I say, stepping up beside Masen.

He's already bent over the engine, poking around.

"Your terminals are corroded."

"That sounds bad," I whisper.

He chuckles and thrusts a hand out behind him. "Come here."

I slip my hand into his, allowing him to tug me closer. Sparks ignite where our skin meets, sending a jolt of electricity up my arm. He feels it too and curses beneath his breath. He doesn't let me go though. He tugs me forward until I'm pressed up against his side, peering under the hood with him.

My heart beats so hard I'm sure he probably hears it.

"You see these right here?" he asks, pointing out two little metal pieces with red and black cables connected to the battery.

"Yes."

"These are the battery terminals."

"Oh."

"They help run power from the battery to the rest of the car. But yours are corroded, so the car isn't getting enough juice. You need to replace them."

"Okay." I shift my weight from one foot to the other. "Um, is it going to be expensive?"

"Nah," he says. "They're not expensive. Watch your fingers."

I move my hands out of the way, shoving them into my pockets.

He slams the hood closed and then turns to face me. "I'll pick up a set tonight and get it taken care of. I'm guessing you need your car for class tomorrow?"

"We're on break until the 5th. I'm working tomorrow."

He jerks his chin in a nod. "I'll take you home."

"You don't have to do that."

"Never said I did, sunflower." His gaze roves across my face, his upper lip ticking up into a half smile. "Come on. Let's get you home."

I don't bother arguing. It won't do me any good. Instead, I circle back to the driver's side and open the door to get my stuff out of the car. He stands behind me, so close I can practically feel the heat of him again. Is he staring at my ass?

My cheeks heat at the thought. But some wicked little part of me has me leaning further into the car, lifting it higher into the air for him. It might be my imagination, but I think I hear him groan. He shifts around behind me as if he's restless.

I bite my lip to hide a smile and back slowly out of the car.

"I'm ready."

When his eyes meet mine, I know he knows what I was doing. He doesn't call me out on it though. He just stares at me for a moment, hunger stamped across every line of his face. And then he shakes his head like he's trying to clear it and takes my bags from me.

His hand slides down the outside of my arm, making me shiver.

We walk in silence to his truck. He stays glued to my side, matching his stride to mine. His legs cover a lot more ground than mine do. I'm five seven, but all my height is in my torso. My legs are ridiculously short.

He holds the passenger door open for me and I'm pretty sure he stares at my ass again while I scramble inside. My foot slips from the step-rail.

"Careful, baby girl," he says, grabbing me before I fall backward onto the cement.

I bite my tongue, fighting the urge to moan at the feel of his hands encircling my waist. I'm not a small girl. I'm lucky if I can squeeze into a size sixteen. But his hands fit the natural curve of my waist like they were made to fit there.

He takes his time lifting me into the truck. By the time my butt lands in the bucket seat, I'm a mess of raw nerves and tingling desire. I don't imagine the way he looks at me this time. Or the way he leans in close.

"You smell so fucking good," he rasps, running his nose down the side of my temple as he pulls the seatbelt tight around me. He's all up in my personal space, his body crowding mine against the seat. His unique scent swirls around me, making my head spin. If I smell half as appealing to him as he does to me, I get why he's currently sniffing me.

The seatbelt clicks into place.

I whimper, unable to stop the sound.

He pulls away, leaving me trembling in the seat. His eyes meet mine again, so much darker than they've ever been before. "You aren't going to the New Year's party with Marco, Theia."

I blink wide eyes at him. "I'm not going with Marco."

"You're going with me."

I blink again. Before I can even process his quiet command, he slams the door between us.

"What in the world?" I mumble, staring blankly. Why does he think I'd go anywhere with Marco? And did he just *order* me to go on a date with him?

I press the heel of my hand to my forehead, trying to rub away the confusion swirling through my mind, but it doesn't help. My entire body hums like a livewire, and every inch of this truck smells like its owner. My thoughts are scattered around like the remnants of a trainwreck.

He climbs into the driver's side, slamming the door behind him.

"Who said I was going to the party with Marco?" I manage to ask.

"Heard a rumor," he mutters, not even looking at me.

"That's a dumb rumor."

"You don't want to go with him?"

"I wouldn't even go to the grocery store with Marco, let alone a New Year's Eve party."

"You don't like him?" Masen cranks the engine.

"I don't even know him," I say, staring at him like he's crazy. He might be if he thinks I have a thing going on with Marco. "We've spoken maybe half a dozen times since he got here. Well, he spoke. He never *stops* speaking. It makes my head hurt."

Masen chuckles. "He does like the sound of his own voice."

"Who said I was going with him?"

"Killian might have mentioned it."

I frown, perplexed as to why Killian would think that. Or why he'd even mention it to Masen. Killian isn't exactly someone who goes around spreading gossip. Honestly, he says less than Masen most of the time. "Well, Killian was wrong," I say, leaning back in the seat. "I'm not going to the New Year's Eve party at all, let alone with Marco."

"You're going with me," Masen says, backing out of the parking spot.

"Is that a question or a demand?"

"Whichever gets you to agree, sunflower," he says, cutting his eyes at me. Even in the dark, the seriousness in them is unmistakable. He wants me to go with him.

"I'll go with you," I whisper.

It might be my imagination, but I think he exhales a little sigh of relief.

CHAPTER FOUR
Masen

Theia is quiet on the drive to her house, but I can practically hear the wheels of her mind turning. The closer we get, the more restless she grows. I bite my lip to hide a smile, waiting her out. I know what she's wondering, why she keeps peeking over at me.

"How do you know where I live?" she finally asks as we pull into the driveway of her complex. The gate is thrown wide open like usual, which bugs me. What's the fucking point of living in a gated complex if anyone can just drive right in with no problem?

"I know a lot of things, sunflower," I say, glancing over at her. Even in the dark, she's the prettiest little angel I've ever seen. She lights up the dark, her aura swallowing up shadows without dimming her light in the least. Does she even know how goddamn perfect she is? How beautiful?

"How?" she demands, not satisfied with my answer. I'm not surprised. Theia is curious about everything, eager to experience all the world has to offer. Nothing escapes her notice. I've been watching her do her job for months now. She's good with everyone because she pays attention, notices the things everyone else misses.

"I've been here before," I say, pulling into the spot outside of her apartment. She's on the bottom floor of the second building, sandwiched between an elderly man with a cocker spaniel and a single mom with a little girl. Her tiny porch is decked out for Christmas, the lights around the door twinkling red and white and green.

"When were you here?" she demands, turning in the seat to gape at me.

I avoid the question, not sure the answer won't get me slapped into the new year. Truth is, I've been here more than once. More often than I think she's prepared to know. She's my peace, my home. When she isn't close, I can't settle.

"Let's get you inside, baby girl," I say, killing the engine instead of answering.

"No."

I unlatch my seatbelt before turning to face her. Light spills into the cab of the truck from the streetlights positioned all around the parking lot. She's got her arms crossed, pushing her breasts up high. The stubborn tilt to her chin makes my dick throb. So does the recalcitrant look in her eyes. Nothing pisses her off more than being ignored. And nothing makes my dick harder than when she's feeling spunky.

She's so soft-spoken most of the time, so shy and sweet. But this other side of her is sexy as hell. She doesn't back down and doesn't surrender. When she wants something, she's fearless. I can't wait to see how that translates once she's in my bed.

"When were you here, Masen?" she asks.

"Yesterday."

Her eyes widen.

"And the day before."

Her lips part.

"Christmas Day too. And Christmas Eve." I pocket the keys, my eyes locked on hers. "I'm here every goddamn day, sunflower."

"Do...do you live here?" she asks, confusion swirling through her expression.

"No. You do."

I climb out of the truck before she can say anything else. It's a chickenshit move, there's no denying that. But if she's freaked out, I'm not ready to face it. And if she's pissed...well, I'm not ready to face that either. The last thing I want to do is frighten this angel. That's not why I come here. I come because I have to. Because wild horses couldn't drag me away from her now.

I circle around the truck slowly to open her door.

She's still in the same position, frozen in shock.

"Come on," I murmur, reaching over her to unlatch her seatbelt. I have to fight the urge to sniff her again. She smells like spring rain and warm vanilla. It's a deadly combination. Every time I lose her scent after being in the daycare, I want to rip shit apart.

She doesn't say a word as I lift her out of the truck, not willing to risk her falling. She trips a lot. Over her own feet. Over thin air. Over nothing and everything. When she wears heels to work, I worry all fucking day that she's going to break her neck chasing after the kids. It's not that she's clumsy either, not exactly. It's more like she's so focused on everyone else that she loses track of herself. There's so much love in this little sunflower.

I grit my teeth as I slide her down my body to her feet, feeling every sexy curve of her body. Christ, touching her without being able to *touch* her is torture. I want to grip her tightly, feel the way her curves mold to my harder frame. I want to back her up against the truck and make her purr.

I reach inside the truck to grab her bags instead.

We walk in silence to her front door. I feel her peeking up at me though, as if checking to see if I know which door is hers. I do. I lead her right to it, stopping beside a three-foot-tall wooden nutcracker soldier, gaily painted in traditional Christmas colors.

She fumbles with the key in the lock for a moment before she manages to unlock the door. "Um, do you want to come in?" she asks, peeking over her shoulder at me.

Yes. More than I want my next breath.

"I shouldn't," I say. "I need to get to the parts store before they close."

"Oh." The disappointment in her expression makes me feel like an asshole and a king at the same damn time. The last thing I want to do is disappoint her, but knowing she wants me to come inside does a number on my cock. "I should give you money."

I shake my head. "I've got it, sunflower."

"You can't pay to fix my car, Masen."

"I can."

She narrows her eyes on me, growling.

I grin in response. She's so fucking cute when she's annoyed. She's a little kitten, playing at being a tiger. I don't think she knows she doesn't need claws to bring me down. One word from her lips could put me on my knees.

"You are so annoying," she complains.

"I come here because you're here," I say before she can launch into a diatribe about me paying to fix her car. As if I wouldn't empty my life savings for her without missing a beat. Everything I have is hers. There isn't much of it, but it's hers, nonetheless.

Her eyes widen again. "What? Why, Masen?"

"Because I'd follow you to hell, Theia," I say, leaning forward to press my lips to her cheek. At least that's my intention—a small taste to hold me over until she's mine. She turns her head at the last second so my lips land against hers instead.

Reality flies away faster than a bullet exiting the chamber.

As soon as I feel her lips touch mine, I lose what little composure I have. Three months, I've been clinging to it with my fingertips, trying like hell to do this right, to be a man worthy of her. One small taste overturns the apple cart, sends my good intentions and my self-control up in smoke.

Her bags hit the ground with a faint thud as I yank her into my arms. She topples into me like the sweetest little treat, her cry of shock, of *relief*, quickly silenced with my lips. I don't kiss her. I devour her like the unruly beast I am, the one desperate for a single second of this angel's attention. I've done a lot of fucked up shit in the name of God and country. I live with those reminders echoing in the back of my mind. But for her? I'd do it all again and wouldn't regret a second of it.

Lust explodes between us like a bomb blast. The remnants of my self-control land at my feet, shattered into fine pieces. And God, it feels good. Kissing her. Touching her. Not fighting every goddamn minute of the day to keep my hands to myself.

I don't keep them to myself now.

I back her up against the wall, touching her everywhere at once. My hands work up and down her body, feeling every curve, every sweet little roll of flesh. Her hands do a little exploring of their own. She pulls my hair, runs her palms down my back, tries to pull me closer.

Her sweet sobs of ecstasy are too much and not enough. I need to know what this angel sounds like when she's coming. That's the only thought in my mind as I boost her up into my arms with my hands on her ass. She wraps her legs around my waist, her head thumping against the wall.

I grip her ass tight, grinding her against my dick as I attack her mouth.

She turns to putty in my arms, melting into me. Her whimpers turn to a sharp cry when the hard ridge of my erection finds her clit. She practically catapults out of my arms in shock before grasping onto my shoulders and dragging herself back down for more.

"Oh, baby girl," I breathe. "Did I find your sweet spot?"

"Yes," she moans. "Do it again, Masen."

"Kiss me, Theia."

She latches onto my lips like an obedient little angel, clinging to my shoulders. Her inexperience is obvious as her mouth works against mine, clumsy and uncertain at first, and then more firmly. She touches her tongue to my bottom lip, questing, eager.

"Fuck," I growl when she follows that up by biting it.

"Sorry."

She's not. I hear it in her voice.

I bounce her against my dick again as she touches her tongue to mine. Destiny is a hell of a thing. My whole life, I thought mine was the Navy. I thought it was killing and fighting and never fucking resting. In her arms, I realize just how wrong I was. This is what I was meant for, what I was born for. Holding her. Kissing her. Protecting her. Making her sing.

She sings now, the sweetest little song of pleasure. Her cries echo in the night before being carried away by the wind. I revel in each moan, each whimper. They burrow deep into my brain, banishing a little bit of the darkness. Old memories, painful memories get swallowed up, replaced with *her*. How good she feels. How sweet she sounds. How tightly her thick thighs lock around my waist.

She comes with a whimper that hits me like a roar. It creates a landslide inside, every tremor claiming more of my heart, of my soul. By the time she falls limp in my arms, whispering my name, every square inch of both belong to her. She lights them up with her sweetness, with her light, and makes them her own.

"Sunflower," I whisper, nuzzling my face into her throat, pressing adoring kisses into her skin. My cock throbs for release, but I've never been more satisfied than I am in this moment. I've got an angel in my arms and her taste on my tongue. Not a fucking thing in the world beats that.

"Mommy! There's a truck parked in Aunty Theia's spot."

"Shit," I whisper, quickly sliding Theia down my body as the little girl's voice grows closer.

Theia stumbles, her legs wobbling beneath her. I wrap my arms around her, pulling her into my embrace. I'm not even close to ready to let her go yet. I just don't want to try to explain to a little girl why I've got her Aunty Theia plastered to the wall with my hands on her ass.

"Aunty Theia!" the little girl cries from behind me a second later. "You're home. Whoa. Your friend is big. What's his name?"

Theia tries to step out of my arms. I reluctantly let her go.

Her wide eyes meet mine, her lips swollen from my kisses, her hair all fucked up from the wall. She looks freshly fucked and too damn beautiful. I thrust my hands into my pockets, fighting the urge to toss her over my shoulder and carry her inside to get her off again.

"Brinley Grace, get back inside right now," a woman calls after the little girl.

"But mommy, there's a man with Aunty Theia," she protests.

A second later, her mom pops her head around the corner. It takes her all of two seconds to assess the situation and realize we were up to no good. She doesn't look pissed that her daughter almost caught us though. If anything, she looks amused as her gaze bounces from me to Theia, who is blushing bright red, and then back to me.

"What's your name?" Brinley asks.

"Masen. Masen Starks."

Her mom's eyes widen like she recognizes my name. Interesting.

"You're big," Brinley says, tipping her head back to look up at me. "Are you a giant?"

"Afraid not, sweetheart," I say, chuckling. She's cute. Maybe four or five, with big green eyes and fiery red hair that matches her mom's. Her mom is curvy like Theia, only about six inches shorter.

"Oh," Brinley says, her face falling in disappointment. "Why were you hugging my Aunt Theia?"

"I was saying bye."

Her mom laughs quietly.

Theia's cheeks turn scarlet.

"Sorry," Brinley's mom says. "She escaped before I could stop her."

"It's fine," Theia says. "Um, Masen, this is Mina and Brinley. Mina, Brinley, this is Masen."

"Hi," Brinley chirps.

"Hey, Masen," Mina says, grinning at me. "Nice to meet you. We'll get out of your hair." She shoots Theia a look that says they'll be talking about this later.

Theia practically squirms on her feet.

"I'm headed to the parts store, sunflower," I murmur, stepping forward to press my lips to her cheek. "What time do I need to pick you up in the morning?"

"You don't have to pick me up. Mina can take me to work."

"What time, baby girl?"

"Seven," she says, rolling her eyes like I'm annoying her.

"I'll be here at seven. Lock your door when you go in." I release her and turn to find Mina and Brinley both watching us.

Mina's grinning ear to ear. Her grin widens when Theia mutters that I'm bossy.

She hasn't even seen bossy yet though. When I get her in my bed, she'll find out exactly how bossy I can be. But I don't tell her that. Not with Brinley and Mina standing right there. Instead, I head to my truck, her taste still in my mouth and her cries still ringing in my ears.

"You brought me breakfast?" she says early the next morning, staring with wide eyes at the paper bag I deposit in her lap.

"You usually eat when you get to work," I say, buckling her into the seat. She looks beautiful today. She's dressed in another pair of jeans and a pretty blue sweater that matches her eyes. It does incredible things to her full breasts too.

"How do you know that?" she asks, gaping at me.

I wink at her and slam the door closed.

"Masen!" she shouts through it. "How do you know that?"

I chuckle and circle around to the driver's side before climbing in. She's got the bag open on her lap, peeking into it.

"I'm not even going to ask how you know Dana's is my favorite bakery," she mumbles, more to herself than to me before she pulls the cheese Danish out of the bag and takes a big bite. She hums her approval, her eyes rolling back in her head.

"Jesus," I mutter, shifting in the seat.

Her gaze comes to mine, her cheeks heating.

I back out of her parking spot and head toward the road, my grip tight on the steering wheel. Now that I know what she tastes like, what she sounds like, keeping my hands off her is going to take every ounce of control I possess.

"You kissed me last night," she blurts halfway to the office.

"I did more than kiss you, sunflower."

"We're not talking about that."

Her prim tone makes me smile. I cast a look in her direction, confirming that her cheeks are red again. She's cute as hell when she's embarrassed.

"Why aren't we talking about it?"

"Because we're not."

My grin widens.

"Shut up," she says, smacking me in the chest when I laugh.

I catch her hand in mine, pulling it up to kiss her fingers.

She groans my name, squirming in the seat.

"You're confusing me," she whispers when I release her hand.

"What's confusing?"

"You. This. *Everything*." She flaps a hand in the air as if to illustrate what she means. "You kissed me, Masen. And you're being all flirty and weird. It's stressing me out."

"You kissed me," I remind her.

"Did not."

"You did."

"Fine, maybe I did," she huffs, peering at me through narrowed, suspicious eyes. "But that's beside the point. You're being weird."

"How so?"

"You're always broody and grumpy. You never flirt with me. You think I'm too young and need a babysitter," she says, scowling at the dashboard.

"You are young, and you do need someone watching out for you."

She growls at me. I think she'd kick me right now if she could.

"You work around men all day, sunflower," I remind her. "Most of them haven't had pussy in longer than they want to admit. They see a sweet little thing like you and start thinking about things they shouldn't."

"Oh," she says and then hesitates for a minute. "Is that why you kissed me? Because you haven't had...um, you haven't slept with anyone in a while?"

"Years."

"What?"

"It hasn't been a while," I say. "It's been years."

"Oh. Why?"

"Theia."

"Stop saying my name like that!" she cries, scowling at me again.

"Like what?"

"*Theia*," she mimics, pitching her voice low. "I'm man, hear me roar."

Fuck, she's cute.

"First, I hope I don't sound like that," I say, chuckling as we come to a stop at a red light not far from the office. Traffic is moving faster than usual this morning. Everyone is still off for the holidays. "Second, you're too goddamn cute when you're feeling feisty. Third, I don't roar."

"You don't answer questions either."

"Because I don't want you thinking about me with other women," I growl. "Doing the shit I did...there wasn't a whole lot of time to chase pussy or fuck around. And I was never interested in a long string of one-night stands. Not all men are like Marco, sunflower. I'm certainly fucking not."

She gapes at me for a second and then her lips curve into a soft smile. "That's the most you've ever said to me at once."

"I don't say much."

"Really? I hadn't noticed."

"Smart ass," I mutter, cutting my eyes in her direction again to find her laughing to herself. "You're awful feisty this morning. Rough night?"

Her smile slips, letting me know I hit the nail on the head. She didn't sleep any better than I did last night. And I didn't sleep a wink. I kept imagining her alone in her bed. I jerked my cock raw in search of relief. What little I found was short lived. As soon as I'd think about her in my arms, he'd pop right back up again.

"Were you thinking about me, sunflower?" I ask, unable to help myself.

"No."

"Theia."

"Were you thinking about me?" she demands instead of giving me what I want.

I don't answer. At least not right away. I pull into the parking lot first, taking the spot beside her car. I got the battery terminals changed last night. Changed her oil and her filters too. I'm not telling her that though. I have a feeling it'll just stress her out.

"There aren't many times when I'm not thinking about you, sunflower," I say once I kill the engine. "You're in my head every fucking minute of the day."

"Oh," she whispers. And then, so soft I almost miss it, "Me too."

CHAPTER FIVE
Theia

"Knock, knock!" Mina calls, popping her head into my apartment. Her green eyes dart around the room as if she's checking to make sure Masen isn't here. When she grins at me, I know that's exactly what she's doing.

"He's not here," I mutter, plopping down on the couch with a dramatic sigh.

"Too bad. Looked like you two were having fun last night," she says, pulling the door closed behind her. She holds a bottle of wine up. "I brought a peace offering." Her face scrunches up. "Had I known you guys were out there, I would have duct-taped Brinley to the chair."

"It's fine," I say and then laugh. Mina is the best mom. Brinley is a spirited little girl. She's always up to something. But Mina takes it all in stride. She loves her daughter like crazy. So do I. Without them to keep me company, I'd be miserable most days. "I'll take the wine though."

She kicks her shoes off and crawls onto the couch with me before passing the bottle over. "You did not tell me Masen was hot as hell."

"Yes, I did," I say, trying to work the wrapper off the neck of the bottle. We're both poor, so the bottle doesn't have a stopper. It's cheap wine. My favorite kind. "I think my exact words were, 'He's hot as hell, Mina.'."

"Well, I was not prepared for you to mean it," she says with a soft laugh.

"Is Brinley with your aunt?"

"Yeah, she's keeping her tonight so I don't have to drive her over there at the ass crack of dawn in the morning before work." Mina pouts. "We both hate getting up early."

"Me too." I twist the cap off the wine bottle and take a drink. It's Moscato, my favorite kind.

"Are you going to tell me what happened or do I have to pry it out of you?" Mina asks, accepting the bottle when I pass it back to her. She takes a drink and then hums her enjoyment before looking at me again. "He definitely wasn't saying goodbye with words from the looks of it."

"He kissed me." I frown. "I kissed him. Whatever. We kissed. And then, um... other stuff happened," I say, hiding my face behind my hands like a dork. As if Mina would judge me. She's been trying to talk me into seducing him for months.

"I knew it!" she cries. "You had sex hair."

"Did not," I mumble.

"You did." She grins at me. "You looked really happy, Theia. So did he."

I peek over the top of my hands. "He did?"

"He couldn't keep his eyes off you," she confirms, smiling at me.

"He told me this morning that he thinks about me all the time," I admit.

"I bet he does," she says, wagging her brows.

"He asked me to the New Year's Eve party."

"If you didn't say yes, I'm not sharing my wine with you anymore."

"I said yes," I say, snagging the bottle from her and making her laugh. I take another drink and then pass it back. "I think he only asked me to keep me from going with someone else."

"You were going with someone else?"

"No." I make big eyes at her. "Killian told him that Marco Alvarez—you know the annoying one I told you about? —yeah, him. Anyway, Killian told Masen that Marco planned to ask me. Which is weird because Marco and I barely even speak. He's not interested in me and I'm definitely not interested in him."

"Maybe Killian made it up," Mina says.

"Why?"

"To get Masen to ask you, obviously," she says with a laugh.

"Maybe." I didn't think of that before, but maybe he did. I'm sure Liberty has probably told him by now that I'm in love with Masen. She figured it out months ago. She doesn't pry though. That's not Liberty's way. She's just quietly there, lending her support. Maybe she mentioned it to Killian though, and he decided to take matters into his own hands. He's not exactly the matchmaking type, but he is the take charge and get shit done type.

"Are you excited?" Mina asks.

"I'm nervous," I confess, taking another sip of wine. "And confused."

"About what?"

"Everything!" I cry, being dramatic again. But seriously. My head hasn't stopped spinning since Masen drove me home yesterday. I feel like I crash landed in a different dimension, one where nothing is what I thought it was.

"I'm so in love with him. But he's waited all this time to make a move. Why now? What changed?"

"He did," Mina says, her voice soft.

I tip my head to the side to look at her.

"You said he's been through a lot," she reminds me. "Maybe he just needed some time to get his head on straight before he made a move. He doesn't strike me as the kind of guy to do things in half measures."

Is that why he kissed me? I don't know. Part of me thinks she's probably right though. The Masen who kissed me last night isn't the same Masen I met six months ago. He's not broken anymore, for one. He smiles now, laughs now. Every day, he seems a little more at peace, a little less like he's fighting just to make it through the day.

"I want to seduce him," I blurt.

"Finally!" Mina cries, throwing her hands up and shimmying her hips.

I toss a throw pillow at her, laughing quietly.

She catches it and sets it to the side. "I'm serious, Theia," she says, tucking strands of hair behind her ears. "You've been in love with him since you met him. Pull out the big guns and go get your man. If you don't take the leap, you'll regret it forever." Her expression twists. "Believe me, I know a thing or two about regret."

I fling my arm around her, squeezing her hard. She's still in love with Brinley's dad, but he disappeared before Brinley was born. I'm not entirely sure what happened because she never talks about it, but he flew to Mexico one day and just...vanished. No one ever heard from him again. It's been five years, and Mina still isn't over him. I want answers for her so badly. It breaks my heart that she'll probably never have them. Americans disappear in Mexico far too often.

"Don't make me weepy," she says, hugging me back. "We have things to do."

"We do?"

"Uh, yeah." She releases me and hops to her feet, holding a hand out for me. "New Year's Eve is in two days. You need a dress."

"I have a dress."

"Does it come in pieces?"

"No."

"Then you don't have the *right* dress," she says, dragging me toward the door. "Luckily for you, I have a dress that's going to send him over the edge. You can thank me by making me your Maid of Honor at the wedding."

"Wedding?" I say...squeak.

"Wedding," she says, throwing the door open. "We're playing hardball."

"Oh boy," I whisper, slightly terrified.

By the time Mina finds the dress in the back of her closet and I try it on, we're both well on the way to tipsy. She tries to talk me into wearing a strappy pair of stilettos with it, but I'm not nearly crazy enough—or drunk enough—to even try. I'd break my neck before I even made it out of the bedroom in them.

The dress is gorgeous though. She wasn't joking when she said it came in pieces. The top is a halter that ties up around my neck. Strategically placed pieces of fabric criss-cross the midsection, showing little flashes of skin. The skirt is slit all the way up the thigh on one side. It's more daring than anything I've ever worn before, but I can't deny that it looks incredible on me.

I can't wait for Masen to see me in it. If it doesn't make him realize that I'm more than old enough for him, nothing ever will.

When I make it back to my apartment, there's a bag of takeout sitting in front of the door. I stumble to a stop, staring at it in confusion. I didn't order food. I turn to look out into the parking lot, but no one else is around.

I creep toward the bag like it's going to bite me. There's a note taped to the top.

Sunflower,

Didn't want to interrupt girl's night but figured you might be hungry. You don't eat enough.

-Mase

I read the note twice, disappointment that I missed him warring with joy that he came to see me and relief that the food isn't a weird sex-trafficking trap or something. I scoop the bag up and then let myself into my apartment, my stomach growling. I have no idea how he knew, but I'm starving. By the time I got home, I just wanted to sit and obsess about Masen, so I didn't eat.

I set the bag down and pull my phone out of my pocket.

Me: Thank you. Also...do you have my apartment bugged?

At this point, I wouldn't put it past him. He knows way too much about my life. That should probably freak me out, but it doesn't. The fact that he pays enough attention to know what I eat and where isn't creepy to me. It's honestly kind of...sexy.

Maybe I'm crazy but a tiny part of me likes the thought of him watching over me. I don't need a babysitter, this much is true. But I don't remind him of that because I don't want him watching out for me. I say it because I want him to see me as a grown woman capable of handling her own life. I want him to see me as someone he could love.

But I think I've had it all wrong. All this time, I've been thinking that he thinks I'm too young for him. I'm beginning to realize that maybe the issue is more that he thinks he's too old for me. There's a distinct, important difference. It's not my inexperience that's the issue. It's everything *he's* been through, his trauma. He doesn't think I'm not enough for him. I think he thinks *he's* not enough for me. As if he could ever be anything less because of his scars and the horrors that haunt his mind. He's a legitimate war hero. I could never, would never judge him for the things he did for our country. They will never make him less than a hero in my eyes.

One way or another, I intend to make him see it too. Starting with seducing him.

I tear into the takeout bag, eager to see what he brought me. The container of street tacos from my favorite restaurant tumbles the rest of my heart into his hands. My mouth waters as the smell of the spices fills my small apartment.

I kick my shoes off and curl up on the couch, already stuffing one into my mouth. My phone dings when I'm halfway through the second.

I quickly shove it in my mouth and grab my phone.

Masen: Theia.

Me: Wow. Even over text you manage to say my name in that tone.

Masen: What tone?

Me: Your bossy tone.

Masen: You haven't seen bossy yet, sunflower.

Me: Is that a threat?

Why do I hope it is? Oh, right. Because he brought me tacos. It's not humanly possible to be annoyed with someone who brings you tacos.

Masen: Depends.

Me: On what?

Masen: On whether or not you're itching for a spanking.

I spill my third taco all down my shirt, my mind tangling with fantasies of him bending me over his knee, his rough hand on my ass as he growls my name.

"And now I need to do laundry," I mumble to myself. I need clean panties. And batteries for my vibrator. I squirm on the couch, desperately wishing he had interrupted girl's night. I want him to kiss me again. And touch me.

Masen: For the record, I plan to be real bossy with you either way, baby girl.

"What is he doing to me?" I groan, and then I reread his text, smiling like a crazy person. Maybe seducing him won't be as hard as I thought it would. Had I known that all it would take to get him to make a move was for him to think I was going somewhere with Marco... Okay, no. Even then, there's not a chance in hell I would have gone anywhere with Marco. Gross.

Besides, I don't want to play some stupid game and make Masen jealous. No one deserves that, least of all him. He's been through enough. I just want him. Period. I love him so damn much.

No one said I can't make him squirm a little though.

Me: You talk a big game, Masen Starks. And yet....

Masen: And yet what?

I can practically hear him growling the question.

Me: And yet I've seen no action.

I don't even have time to take a bite before my phone rings.

I squeak, dropping my taco back into the container.

"How drunk are you right now, sunflower?" he growls as soon as I swipe to answer.

"That depends."

"On...?"

"How grumpy you are right now. Because if you're grumpy, then I'm wasted, and this conversation definitely has to wait until later," I say, picking chicken off my taco and popping it into my mouth.

"Yeah? And if I'm not grumpy?" The smile in his voice makes my whole body weak. No, I don't want to make him jealous. I want to be the reason he smiles every damn day of his life.

"Then I'm only a little tipsy," I say, licking juice from my fingers.

"Did you eat your dinner?"

"Did you bug my apartment?"

"No."

"Then how did you know I was craving tacos?"

"You love tacos."

"How did you know I was drinking?"

"Your friend almost caught you writhing all over my cock last night, sunflower," he says with a chuckle I feel deep in my belly. "I may not know much about dating, but I know damn well that things like that require conversations and giggling. And women always bring wine to talk about men."

I mean, he's not wrong.

"I could have eaten already," I point out, though I have no idea why. I just can't resist needling him. It's driving me crazy that he won't tell me how he knows everything about me. Does he think I'll flee into the night if he tells me?

"You don't eat enough."

"My thighs beg to differ."

"Don't," he growls. And whoa. My girly bits literally tingle at the harsh sound. "You're so goddamn beautiful it hurts to look at you, Theia. Don't ever doubt that."

There's so much heat in his tone. It's almost like he believes what he just said so strongly the power of his conviction bleeds through the phone, compelling me to believe it too.

"I know my weight doesn't define me," I say quietly, letting him know I mean it. "I'm not self-conscious about my body. I was just teasing."

"Good because you shouldn't be. Your curves are sexy as hell."

"Thank you."

"You're blushing right now, aren't you?"

"No." I totally am but I'm not telling him that. He already sounds smug. The sexy, infuriating, confusing, hot, beautiful jerk. "Why are you calling me?"

"To make sure you finished your dinner before I give you what you want and make you come."

Oh. My. Gosh.

"Are you finished eating?"

I am now.

"Yes," I whisper.

"Are you in your bedroom or the living room?"

"Living room."

"Go get ready for bed, sunflower. But don't hang up."

"I..."

"Go."

I'm on my feet before my mind can even process the fact that I *want* to obey him. I leave the container of tacos on the coffee table before scurrying toward the bathroom. He doesn't speak as I undress, but I can hear him breathing and rustling around. It makes me feel like he's in the room with me, that intense gaze riveted to every move I make.

"I need to mute you."

"Why?"

"Because you aren't allowed to listen to me pee."

"Hurry then, baby girl."

I mute the phone and take care of business. And then decide to brush my teeth after I wash my hands. My dentist would be horrified at how quickly I scrub them and then spit and rinse.

"Done," I say, a little breathless.

"Good girl."

I whimper, aching at the praise. I never imagined how sexy hearing it could be, or how badly it could make me want to behave just to hear it again.

"Go to bed, sunflower," he says, his deep voice hypnotic.

I stumble obediently to my bedroom and climb into the bed. He's not even here and I'm so worked up, I'm trembling. It's like my body remembers exactly how he made me feel last night and is desperate to experience it again.

"I'm in bed."

He hums his approval and I want to purr like a kitten.

"Are you naked, baby girl?"

"No."

"What are you wearing?"

"Um, a t-shirt and panties."

"Put the phone on speaker and set it beside you."

I accidentally hit a button before I manage to put it on speaker phone.

"Slip your hand into your panties, Theia. Tell me how wet you are for me."

I squirm, my heart thundering in my chest. That voice... he could talk me straight into hell with that voice and I wouldn't even hesitate to follow him through the fire. I slip my hand beneath the covers and into my panties, groaning when my fingers slide through a pool of arousal.

"You're dripping, aren't you?"

"Y-yes."

"Good girl," he croons. "Touch yourself, Theia. Imagine it's my hand. My fingers, touching your slit. My thumb, running in circles around that hard little clit. I'm the one who decides how fast to make you come...or how slow."

"Masen," I groan, my back arching off the bed.

"I want it slow, sunflower. I want you shaking before you come for me."

"Please," I gasp.

"Slow, baby girl. Don't make me tell you again."

"Oh, God."

"No. Not God. He didn't guard you close enough, sunflower. He let you waltz out of heaven and into my path. You say my name when I'm making you come, you understand?"

"Masen." I'm not sure if I'm agreeing, pleading, or dying. Every word from his lips makes my clit throb. My nipples too. I've never felt like this when touching myself. It's a little terrifying how badly I need to come right now.

"Good girl," he croons. "When you touch yourself, do you put your fingers in that juicy little hole, Theia?"

"S-sometimes."

"Good. Do it now."

I circle my opening and then slip two fingers inside, moaning his name.

"One more, baby girl," he says. "You can take it."

Except I can't. I know I can't.

"Do it, Theia," he growls.

"What are you doing to me?" I cry, doing exactly like he demanded and working a third finger inside. I'm so wet I know he can hear the squelch as I work them in and out. I want him to hear it. I hope it makes him ache like I am. I hope it makes him squirm like I am.

"Ruining you, sunflower. Fuck yourself with your fingers nice and slow."

I do, moaning his name loud and then louder. I writhe on the bed, my purple sheets tangling around my legs. My pillow slips off the side onto the floor. The mattress shifts and creaks as I give him exactly what he wants, so far under his spell I feel like he's right here with me. He's the one thrusting into me, filling me again and again. He's the one who has my back arching and sweat sliding down my skin.

"Please, Masen," I plead, desperate to come. "Please."

"Poor little sunflower," he croons. "Do you need to come?"

"Yes!"

"Do it, baby girl. Use your thumb to play with your clit. Don't try to hold back your cries like you had to last night. I want to hear them. Tell me how good you feel."

"S-so good," I sob, pressing my thumb to my clit. That's all it takes to send me over the edge... that and his voice whispering in the dark. I cry out his name, shouting it into the room as the orgasm crashes over me, dragging me down into a riptide of ecstasy. I let it take me, let the waves crash over my head again and again.

And then I hear it. The hitch in his breath. The decadent groan of pleasure.

"Theia. Fuck, Theia."

He's coming too.

Another orgasm sparks, sending me freewheeling into bliss. If this isn't heaven, I don't know how that holy place could possibly compete. Because this? This is where I want to spend eternity.

"Masen," I whisper, collapsing onto the bed and panting for breath.

"Sweet dreams, sunflower," he whispers back.

"Wait."

"What is it?"

"Why did you stay?" I ask, the one question I really want answered. The one that drives me crazy every moment of the day. Why didn't he leave when he finished the pro-gram? Why is he still here?

"Where else would I go, sunflower?" he asks, his voice soft. "So long as you're here, my soul is."

"Masen," I whisper, a powerful swell of emotion tight-ening my throat. Tears pool in my eyes. I hear the truth echoing down the line, more powerfully than his conviction when he said that I'm beautiful. He means it. He stayed because of me.

"I'll see you Friday, baby girl."

"Masen?"

"Yeah."

I love you.

"I'm glad you stayed."

He sighs my name and then disconnects.

For a long time, I stare up at the ceiling, just...allowing myself to feel. His truth. Hope. Joy. For the first time since my dad died five years ago, I don't feel alone anymore. I don't fall asleep alone. Even though Masen is in his own bed miles away, I fall asleep tangled up in him.

Chapter Six
Masen

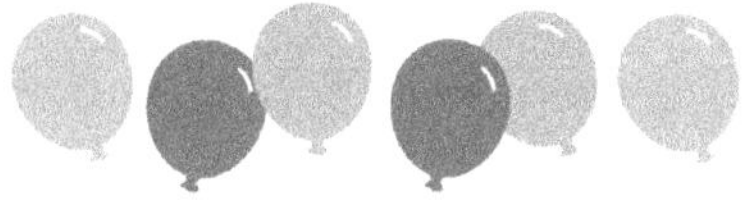

"Coming!" Theia calls from inside her apartment, the sweet sound of her voice making me smile. Hell, who am I kidding? Everything about her has me reacting the same way. I'm addicted to this woman something fierce.

She didn't work yesterday, and the offices were closed today. I haven't seen her since Wednesday. I'm going out of my fucking mind with impatience. It took every ounce of strength I had to keep from driving over here last night to watch her get herself off. We had phone sex again instead.

If I'm not inside her soon, I'm not going to be responsible for the damage I cause. I've wanted a lot of shit in my life. Growing up the way I did, all I did was want—family, a home, normalcy. After Sudan, I would have traded any-thing to go back and do it over. To be the hero people call me and to get those kids out of there safely. But nothing compares to how goddamn badly I want this sunflower splayed out on my bed while I'm fucking my way into her soul.

She already owns mine. I plan to possess hers too.

She texted me a few times today...mostly to ask me how I know so much about her. We both know the answer to that question though. I think she just wants to hear me admit that I've been stalking her for months. I plan to tell her. But not until she sees the house.

I need her to know that I can provide for her. That she'll be safe with me.

I didn't know her daddy. But I know how fiercely she loves him and how intensely she misses him. I'm guessing he was the kind of man who wanted the best for his daugh-ter. I intend to give her that. Every fucking day for the rest of her life.

I spent most of the day out at the house, trying to hurry shit along. I've been pissing off the contractor since I hired him, but I don't give a fuck about that. This is a job to him. It's my entire future. This is where Theia will spend the rest of her life. I'm not willing to accept anything less than perfection for her.

She grew up constantly in motion, moving from base to base. Like me, she never stayed in one place for long. She never had a chance to put down roots and watch them grow. I see the longing in her eyes when she looks at Liberty and Killian. She wants that life for herself so badly...someone to grow old with, somewhere to grow old. I'll move heaven and hell to give it to her, regardless of how the contractor feels about it.

I've rushed every part of the process that can be rushed, greasing palms along the way. But we're still a solid two months from completion. I can't wait two months to make her mine. I was done for the first time I touched her. For months, I've been holding myself in check, trying to do this right. That ship sailed as soon as she kissed me.

By the time the clock strikes midnight tonight, she will be mine in every way.

The chain on the door rattles as she works to unlock it. I take a breath...only to lose it a second later when she throws the door open wide. Every ounce of air in my lungs just vanishes. Every thought in my head goes with it.

Cum shoots up my shaft, my balls pulsing so hard it hurts.

"Jesus Christ," I wheeze, trying not to lose it like a four-teen-year-old boy right here on her doorstep.

Her blonde ringlets cascade from an elegant bun, wispy pieces framing her beautiful face. Her smoky eyes and red lips captivate me. So do the little flashes of her body through her strappy dress. Gone is the sweet angel who makes my dick hard just by existing. In her place stands a goddess ready to bring me to my knees. And God help me, I'm going to let her.

She's got me by the cock, and she knows it. I see the seeds of womanly satisfaction sprouting in her gaze. It tips her lips up into a smile that send sweat trickling down my back.

"Happy New Year, Masen," she says, looking up at me through her lashes. Even dressed like a goddess, she's still my shy little sunflower, stretching eagerly toward what she wants. Her gaze roves down my body, taking in my black tux. Heat creeps into her cheeks, staining them pink. "I've never seen you in anything but jeans and a t-shirt before. You look handsome."

"Come here," I say, holding out a hand for her.

She grasps it, letting me pull her over the threshold and into my arms. I wrap them around her, tucking her right up against my chest where she belongs. My dick nudges her belly, pulling a gasp from her lips.

"Don't pretend that wasn't what you wanted to happen, baby girl," I whisper, placing my lips next to her ear. "We both know you wore that dress specifically to make him hard, didn't you?"

"Maybe," she whispers back.

"If you want to play dirty, I'll let you play," I say, running my hand down to squeeze her plump ass. It looks incredible in her dress. Fuck. I'm going to lose my fucking mind when everyone else sees her dressed like this. There will be no keeping the horny motherfuckers out of the daycare after tonight. That's all right though. They'll know she's mine when she's got my ring on her finger and that belly is swollen with my kid. "Do your worst. Break me. Make it hurt. But when you're done, sunflower? Then it's my turn to do whatever I want to do to you."

"W-what do you want to do to me?"

I palm her ass, pulling her up against me until her tits are crushed against my chest. Until I know she feels every ridge of my cock against her belly. Until my lungs are full of her scent and more of those painful memories crack and fall away.

"Make you my new little plaything," I growl in her ear before nipping her lobe. "But don't worry, baby girl. You'll love every minute of it."

"Masen," she whimpers, trembling like a little doe. She's not afraid though. I hear the desire in her voice—the stark need. She wants it as badly as I do.

Fuck, I'm not going to survive this party.

"Oh, Theia," Liberty says, pulling my sunflower into a hug about an hour into the night. "You look so beautiful."

"Thank you," Theia says, returning her warm embrace.

"Masen." Killian lifts his chin in a nod, as somber as ever. I see the glint in his eyes though. The fucker. He knew damn well that Marco had no intention of asking Theia to the party tonight. I'm not even mad though. Hell, I'm grateful.

"Killian," I say, holding out my fist for him to bump. "The place looks good."

"It does, doesn't it?" Killian says, looking around.

Somehow, the decorator turned the rec hall into a ball-room for tonight. Black curtains cover the walls, with gold and black balloons everywhere. Cheerful gold letters on the back wall spell out a welcome to the new year. The tables scattered around the room are full of the men currently working through the program, their dates, staff, and friends and family. Elegant black and gold centerpieces sit at the center of each table. The bar dominates the back of the room, with two overflowing tables of food on each side. The band plays on a platform at the front, the center of the room reserved for the dancefloor.

It's a helluva lot more effort than a lot of these guys have seen in years. The mood in the room is high. Even those still struggling to adjust to civilian life are enjoying them-selves. Most are chatting in groups. A few have ventured onto the dancefloor with their dates.

I take a step closer to Theia when I see how many of them are looking in our direction. They've been staring since I escorted her inside. She looks too damn beautiful. I've never seen her glow like she is tonight.

If ever I needed proof of how she feels about me, it's this. Seeing her lit up like she's never been this happy before. Seeing the smile on her face, and the softness in her eyes every time she looks at me. She's been giving me hell since we got here, doing everything in her power to bring me to my knees.

War did its damndest to break me. Even at my lowest point, it didn't succeed. I clung to honor by the skin of my teeth. An hour of Theia in this fucking dress and I'm sweating. Antsy. My skin is too tight. My dick is ready to break in half. It's taking everything I have not to take her to the floor and eat that juicy cunt in front of God and everyone.

Liberty whispers something in her ear that makes her laugh.

I slide my arm around her waist, pulling her up against me from behind. She melts into me, pressing her ass against my cock. And goddamn. I can't wait to slip between those cheeks and show her how good I can make that little hole feel.

"You look good, Mase," Liberty says, smiling at me.

"I look lucky," I correct, pressing my lips to Theia's temple. Can't help it. Now that I'm free to touch her, I can't stop. I don't care who sees us or what they think. Every damn one of them wishes they were me right now. They never will be, not if I have anything to say about it.

Theia really is playing with fire tonight. She tips her hips back further, brushing her ass against the head of my cock. It's not accidental either. She does it again, more firmly this time.

I damn near bite my tongue off, trying to fight off a groan.

"Yeah, you do," Liberty says with a laugh. "That dress is fire."

That dress belongs on my bedroom floor.

"I love this dress," Theia sighs dramatically.

I splay my hand across her belly, subtly grinding my dick against her ass. Two can play this game of hers. Though

I'm not going to lie, I'm already on the verge of break-ing. Everything about her acts like an aphrodisiac on my system, overloading it with competing desires. I want to worship at her feet in one breath, and then tie her to the bed and fuck her dirty the next.

Her breath grows choppy, her head lolling on my shoul-der.

I nuzzle her neck, aching to close my teeth around the pulse fluttering in the side of her throat. It pounds just beneath her soft skin, captivating me. There's something sexy as hell about it.

"He's luckier than Marco," Killian says drily, nodding his head at the dance floor.

I follow his gaze, immediately spotting what he means. Marco's standing in the middle of it with a bottle blonde. She throws her hands up in the air and shouts something before her heel comes down on top of his boot. Before anyone can even react, she storms off. Marco gapes after her like he doesn't know what just happened.

He probably doesn't. No one ever accused him of being bright.

"Marines," I mutter.

Killian snorts laughter. "Muscles are required, intelli-gence not essential."

"Killian," Liberty says, trying not to laugh. Killian was a Marine. He's also smart as hell. Marco, on the other hand....

"We're just teasing, baby girl," he says, giving his wife one of his rare smiles.

"You should behave, you know," Theia says, sending a mischievous look over her shoulder that she'll definitely be paying for later. "He's your brother. The Marines are technically part of the Navy, after all."

"We don't claim them," I say, deadpan.

Killian chuckles again, unoffended, and then catches sight of something on the opposite side of the room. He slides his arm around Liberty's waist. "Sebastian and Rowan are here."

"Oh! Let's go say hi." She smiles brightly at me and Theia. "Have fun, you two."

"Bye, Liberty," Theia says. "Bye, Killian."

I rake my teeth down the side of her throat.

"Masen," she moans.

"You having fun trying to break me, sunflower?"

"Yes."

Of course she is.

I smile, pressing my lips to her throat. "Let's go dance then."

CHAPTER SEVEN
Theia

"You know how to dance," I say, swaying in Masen's arms.

"Surprised?" He cocks a brow.

"Not really," I admit, staring up at him. He looks so damn handsome tonight, and so happy. Not a single shadow clings to him. It's as if he's banished the last of them. I know that's not how PTSD works and that he'll always struggle in some ways. But for the first time since I met him, he isn't in pain. For once, he's free. It looks good on him.

"You're like freaking MacGyver. Of course you can dance too." I'm honestly more surprised that *I* can dance. In heels no less. It's his doing. I don't feel clumsy in his arms. I feel graceful, elegant. Following his lead is effortless. "Is there anything you can't do?"

"Get you out of that dress, apparently," he mutters, his expression hot as his hands quest down my back, leaving chills in their wake. "How many times did you trip getting into it, sunflower?"

"None."

"Oh?"

"Maybe one." More like three, but I'm not telling him that. The bruises forming on my knees will tell the story for me. Who makes toilets so low to the ground anyway?

He chuckles, running his nose along my temple. "Every man in here wants to be me right now."

"Yeah?"

"Mmhmm."

"I'm pretty sure all the women want to be me right now too," I say, scrunching up my nose at the thought.

"Jealous?" he asks, pulling back to look at me.

"Are you?" I demand instead of answering even though I'm sure he can probably read the truth on my face. I am jealous that other women are looking at him. Maybe that's not a good thing, but I don't care. I don't want to share even the tiniest piece of him.

"Every man in this room is a hero," he says, pulling me closer. His lips brush my ear, his voice turning to a growl.

"And I want to put every fucking one of them in the ground for looking at you. I'm not simply jealous. I'm fucking rabid with it."

"Me too," I whisper, my stomach clenching at his honesty. He might not say much most of the time, but when he does speak, he holds nothing back. "But you probably shouldn't kill anyone. Jail doesn't sound like much fun. Besides, I only wore this dress to seduce you."

"You're never wearing it again."

"Bossy."

He spins me effortlessly around the floor for a moment, just staring at me. I get caught up in his gaze and the emotion there. There are no shadows, true. But they're still dark, full of wicked thoughts that pull a shiver out of me. He notices and tugs me even closer, seaming our bodies together until there's not even a breath of space between us.

"Why did you want to seduce me?"

"Because I thought you thought I was too young for you," I murmur, running my hands through his hair. It's longer than it was when we met, a little unruly. I love the way it feels between my fingers. "But I realized something."

"Yeah? What's that?" How he can be entirely focused on what I'm saying while running his hands all over me and dancing, I don't know. But he stares at me so intently I know he's memorizing every word. It's not hard to see why he was a SEAL. Captain America has nothing on him.

"I had it all wrong," I say. "It was never about me. It's always been about you not feeling like enough for me, hasn't it?"

"I'm not nearly good enough for you, sunflower," he says, completely serious. "You're pure light, and I'm the motherfucker who wants to drag you into the dark and teach you shit that should shame me." He swallows hard. "But I realized something too."

"What?" I whisper.

"I'm not ashamed." The truth reflects like stars in his eyes, glittering and bright. "You can handle me, can't you, sunflower? You want the same things I do."

"Yes." So bad. I want things from him that I'm not sure I know how to put into words. Things I'm not sure a virgin should want. But when I think about him making love to me, it's rough and hard and so damn good. He isn't sweet and gentle, not always at least. He's a beast...and I'm his willing prey.

"I know you do."

We're not even dancing at this point. We're just standing in each other's arms, swaying. I don't know what song is playing, if it's fast or slow. There's no one else in the room but the two of us. Everyone else ceased to exist long ago.

But I don't want to be here anymore. I don't want to ring in the New Year in this room, celebrating with everyone we know.

When the clock strikes midnight, I want to be in his bed. I want to be his.

"Masen? I'm almost done playing," I say.

He stops swaying, his eyes heating. "Oh yeah?"

I press up against him to steady myself and then lift up on my toes, placing my mouth at his ear. "It's almost your turn to do whatever you want to do to me," I whisper, feeling naughty and daring and exactly like the goddess he thinks I am.

He growls my name, his hands tightening around my waist.

A surge of satisfaction courses through me, making me bolder. If this is my last chance to make him sweat tonight, then I want to make it worth it. I slip one hand between us, letting it brush against his erection. I bite him at the same time, feeling his skin between my teeth, his masculine taste on my tongue.

"Goddamn," he growls, his body vibrating against mine.

I touch his erection again, confident no one can see what I'm doing. The hard length fascinates me. It's been like that all night, and yet he hasn't uttered a single complaint. He hasn't tried to hurry me along. He's let me have my fun, let me tease him.

I tease him mercilessly now, touching him through his pants, exploring. With him, I'm not a shy virgin, unsure of what to do. With him, I'm powerful, confident, and eager. I let instinct guide me as I torment him, captivated by the way he responds. If it weren't for the music, I'm sure everyone would hear the predatory growl rumbling in his throat. If not for the semi-darkness, they'd see the molten desire in his eyes. The warning.

He doesn't have to say a word for me to know I'm going to pay for this later. His eyes scream that truth at me. It doesn't slow me down. I haven't had a drop to drink all night, and yet I feel intoxicated. My reservations are gone, stripped off and discarded on the dance floor. His confession did that. He's afraid to drag me down into the dark with him, but he doesn't have to drag me anywhere. I'll take the first steps myself. Heck, I'll *run* if it leads me to him.

"Baby, baby please," he groans, breaking when I squeeze him through his pants. His body trembles against mine, sweat dotting his brow. "Ah, God, sunflower. You're killing me."

Triumph roars through me, making me giddy.

"Then make me yours, Masen," I demand. "I need you."

He doesn't make me say it again. Between one breath and the next, he changes. My steadfast SEAL turns from patient lover to unruly beast. He releases me just long enough to grab my arm, and then we're moving through the crowd, his steps impatient.

People try to speak to us as we go, but he ignores them all. We leave a trail of knowing laughter in our wake, but I don't care. I'm not ashamed of a single thing about him. I won't be ashamed of the way I want him, nor of the way he wants me. What woman doesn't want to be the sole focus of her man's desire?

Cool air hits me when he pulls me out the doors. The roar from inside fades as they swing closed behind us. And then he makes his move. Before I even know what hit me, I'm pressed up against the wall, his hand around my throat. He doesn't squeeze. He simply holds me still.

"I should make you finish what you started right here," he growls in my ear, pressing up against me. He grinds his erection against my stomach, taking my mouth in a hot kiss. "Goddamn, Theia."

"You..." I gasp when he bites my lip, leaving a sting behind. "You said I could play."

"I'm not going to make it back to your place, sunflower. You've got my dick hurting."

"Take me to your room."

He hesitates, groaning.

"Please," I whisper. "I don't care if it's just a dorm room. I need you!"

I'm not joking. He's been touching me all night. Staring at me. Kissing on my neck. I'm a bundle of raw nerves and pulsing desire. Every time my heart beats, my clit throbs. Every time he breathes, my womb clenches. Teasing him in a room full of people only amplified the desire, increasing it ten thousandfold.

He groans again and then gives in, practically peeling me away from the wall. I don't have to try to keep up with him this time. He swings me up into his arms, carrying me bridal-style. I cling to his shoulders, marveling at how strong he is, at how easily he holds me. He makes it seem effortless.

Neither of us speak as we cut across the parking lot toward the west wing of the building where his room is located. I've seen the dorms before, and I know they aren't much. Everyone has their own private bedroom and bathroom, but that's about it. The kitchens and living spaces are communal.

Somehow, he manages to open the door and hold onto me at the same time. His boots hit the gleaming hardwood floors with solid thumps as he sets off down the long hallway. This place used to be an old hospital, but Killian and Liberty have worked hard to make it something new. To make it feel like a safe place for those who need it most. Decorative lamps replace the harsh overhead lights, giving the dorms a warm glow. Soothing artwork adorns the walls. Antique tables hold vases of flowers and stacks of books and magazines.

Masen charges down the long hallway, the common rooms passing in a blur. We turn right and then left, coming out into a short hallway with four doors, two on each side of the hall. He opens the first on the left, carrying me inside.

Like the rest of the rooms, his is simple, functional. The hardwood floors from the hall give way to simple blue-gray carpet, the same found in hotels the world over. The walls are a deeper shade of blue than the hallway, but it's more obvious here that this used to be a hospital. The windows and air conditioner beneath are distinctive. So are the metal tracks on the ceiling that used to house a privacy curtain. A double bed rests against one wall. An entertainment center with a small television is situated across from it. The far side of the room contains a small table and two chairs. The only other piece of furniture is a dresser.

Aside from a few items neatly arranged on top of the dresser, there are no personal touches. The art on the wall is the same that hangs in every other room. There are no family photos, no trinkets sitting out. There's nothing of him in this room. It's as if he never settled in, never made it his own. All these months, he's just been existing here.

"It's not a home, sunflower," he says as if reading my mind.

"It's your home."

He shakes his head, lowering me to my feet. "This is just where I sleep at night," he says, his eyes boring into me. "You're my home."

"Masen," I whisper.

"You've been home to me since the day I met you."

"You're my home too. My happy place. My favorite part of the day is when you come and see me in the daycare," I admit. "I feel like I can breathe again when you step through the doors."

"That's because you know you're mine."

"I am yours."

"Show me, Theia."

"Show you what?"

"Everything," he growls. "Strip."

CHAPTER EIGHT
Masen

The excitement in Theia's eyes sets fire to my soul, sending it up in a whoosh of flame. If she's nervous, she doesn't show it. She takes a step away from me and then another.

I palm my cock, staring openly at her curvy body in that fucking dress, at the flashes of her soft skin that taunted me all night. She's pure sex and she knows it.

I love that about her. She isn't fragile or insecure. She's wise beyond her years, content with who she is and her place in life. Her father was the one enlisted, but the military forged her spine from steel too. She's no delicate, shrinking flower. She's a fucking warrior. A sunflower, standing tall.

She carefully kicks her heels off, holding onto the side of the entertainment center to keep her balance. Even then, she wobbles to the side, making my heart pulse with soft emotion. How she makes me want to fuck her raw and cradle her close at the exact same time, I don't know.

Once her heels are off, she reaches for the hem of her dress, gliding her hand up her exposed thigh. All night long that fucking slit in her dress taunted me. It climbs right up to her pussy, exposing every inch of her thick thigh but not a single peek of whatever she's wearing beneath. I'm a desperate man, willing to do unspeakable acts just to know what those panties look like. Just to smell her cream on them.

She lifts it slowly, her cheeks flushed pink. Despite her shyness, she keeps her eyes locked on my face, watching me as intently as I do her. The dress creeps up, one excruciating inch at a time. I lock my legs in place, trying to keep myself from lunging at her and ripping it down the middle.

She gathers the silky fabric up in her hands, shimmying her hips as she works it up over them. As soon as I see the pale flesh of her ass, I see red. All fucking night, she's been in that dress with no panties, her pussy inches from making a grand entrance.

"Where are your panties, sunflower?" I growl, stomping toward her.

"In my underwear drawer," she says, far too casually.

I wrap my hand carefully around her throat, gently forcing her head back until her eyes are locked on mine. "Why isn't my pussy covered, baby girl?"

"Does it look like this dress was made for panties, Masen?" she asks, not giving an inch. Of course she doesn't. She knew exactly what she was doing when she decided not to wear panties. She wanted to break me.

I was right earlier. She may be pure light, but she belongs in the dark with me. I've been trying like hell to keep her pure and innocent. I'm not trying anymore. I'll take her where she's itching to go.

I release my hold on her to help work the dress off over her head. It lands in a heap at our feet. I take a step back, devouring every inch of her. Her strapless bra lifts her breasts high, clinging to her like a second skin.

"Goddamn, Theia," I whisper, swallowing hard. I've been to more places than I can count. I've seen beauty and horror and things that convinced me long ago that God absolutely exists. Not even the most beautiful of those places competes with the sight of her standing here right now. She's the prettiest little sunflower, all porcelain skin, and voluptuous curves. "You're beautiful, baby girl."

"You make me feel beautiful," she whispers, smiling shyly.

I scoop her up in my arms, impatient to see her spread across my bed. I've fucked my hand to fantasies of her in this room so many times, certain she'd never set foot over the threshold. She deserves better. I'll never believe different. But she's here now. She's mine now.

I lay her out on the bed, taking her lips in a deep kiss. She moans into my mouth and twines her arms around my neck, locking her body to mine. We fight for control of the kiss, her refusal to submit making my dick hard and then harder still. She finally submits with a whimper.

I slip my tongue into her mouth, twining it around hers. She writhes beneath me, back arched, legs sliding back and forth as she tries to create friction between them. I don't let up until she's panting, breathing little whimpers into my mouth.

Once she's squirming, I break away from her mouth, reaching out to strip her bra off. The sticky fabric peels away from her skin easily, revealing her to my gaze. Her tits should be a national treasure. They're pretty little globes with the sweetest cherries on top.

I pinch one, making her cry out.

"Roll over," I demand, tapping her hip.

She rolls onto her side and then over onto her back.

"Ass in the air, sunflower." I grip her wide hips, staring at her ass. It's been taunting me for months, begging me to touch it, kiss it...fuck it. She's not ready for that yet. But that ass will be mine too. Every part of her will be.

She shifts around, silently getting up on her hands and knees.

"Good girl," I croon, running my hands all over her ass.

She moans and rocks back into my touch, practically purring.

"Masen!" she shouts, her head flying back when I smack her right cheek. My dick throbs in my pants at the sight of it jiggling and bouncing.

"That's for not wearing panties under that dress, Theia," I growl, rubbing away the sting. And then I smack her left cheek. My palm stings as it connects with her flesh.

She cries out my name, her voice thick with pleasure. I only intended to give her the first two slaps, but when she rocks back, eager for more, I spank her again. And then again. Each time, the crack as my hand lands against her flesh echoes and her flesh jiggles and bounces. My blood boils with need.

I lean forward and thrust my hand into her hair, craning her head back.

The sweetest whimper of surrender escapes her lips as her eyes meet mine. Her pupils are dilated, pleasure turning the irises dark. She's so fucking sexy.

"I won't share you, Theia," I murmur. "Not even a part of you."

"I won't share you either!" she cries.

"You think I'd let you?" I run my hand down the crevice of her ass, feeling her wetness against my fingertips. "You're my light, Theia. You're the one who pulled me out of the dark. I'm yours, sunflower. I'll only ever be yours."

"Masen," she whimpers.

I spread her cheeks to play with her asshole.

She gasps, falling forward as her arms lose strength. I think she's shocked. She won't be for long. There will be no secrets between us, no part of her I don't know intimately. This woman is my future, the center of my world. Love isn't a strong enough descriptor for the way I feel about her. It's more powerful than that.

"I told you, baby girl," I remind her, running my thumb all around that puckered hole. "I'm going to do all sorts of filthy shit to you. If you don't like something, all you have to say is no, understand?"

"Yes."

"Do you want to say no?"

"No," she moans.

I reward her by cupping her pussy in my free hand. Her sticky cream soaks my hand, her heat searing me. I want in her so fucking bad it's torture. But I'm not done playing with her yet. She had her fun at that fucking party. It's my turn now.

I play with her asshole and her hard little clit at the same time, watching the way she quivers at my touch. Her cries fill the small room, blanketing it with her sweetness, with her light. I sweated my way through countless nights here, countless nightmares, reliving the moment we were ambushed over and over again. Until it felt like those memories were embedded in the walls here, as if this room was stained with the grief and guilt and pain.

Having her here like this, listening to her breathy cries, watching her trembling body...it changes things. The ghosts of the past lie quietly, releasing their grip. For the first time since I stepped foot over the threshold nearly seven months ago...I stop hating this room. For the first time, I find beauty between these four walls. I find peace.

I play with her until she's pleading for release, and then I stop.

The keening cry of loss rips at my heart, demanding I fix it.

"On your back, Theia," I demand. "Arms up and legs spread."

I have to help her obey my command. She's a whimpering mess, my poor little virgin. I lay her out on the bed, running my hand down her side to soothe her. Once she's settled, I take a step back and strip. Her eyes track every move I make.

I love the way she looks at me. I never gave a fuck what anyone thought about me before her. Didn't care if they liked me, the way I looked, the things I said, or anything else. The only people who mattered were my teammates. I care what this little sunflower thinks. I want her to take pleasure in my body. It'll be the only one she ever sees, ever touches.

"You like watching me, Theia?"

"Yes," she whispers.

I wrap my fist around my shaft, stroking it for her. Her lips part, her expression glassy as she watches me. She shifts on the bed, so hot for it she's shaking.

"I want to tie you down, sunflower. Are you going to let me?"

Her gaze flies back to mine as I pick up my necktie from the end of the bed, dangling it from my free hand.

"I won't hurt you," I vow, meaning it to my soul. I may be rough with her, but she has the power here. She has the control. I'd crawl through glass to worship at her feet.

"I'm not afraid." She licks her lips, the pulse in her throat jumping. "I...just. I'm a virgin, Masen. I don't know...I don't know if that changes anything," she whispers.

"You think I didn't know that?" I smile, amused. There's no way anyone else has ever touched her. If they had, she wouldn't be here right now. She'd belong to some other motherfucker. Thank God no one else ever caught her eye. I don't know why she chose me when she could have anyone, but I'll be thanking God for the rest of my life that she did.

"How did you know?"

"I know you, Theia."

"How?"

"I watch you," I admit, still stroking my cock. "At work. At your place. I follow you around like a lovesick puppy."

"Why?" she whispers.

"Because I can't fucking help it," I growl, narrowing my eyes on her. "Day one, you looked up at me with those big blue eyes like I was something special and knocked me on my ass. My heart was yours right then and there, Theia. I had to be where you are, had to know you were okay. Being near you kept me alive, sunflower. You brought me back from hell."

"Masen," she whispers.

"That's not the only reason," I say before she thinks I'm a gentleman. I'm not. "I did shit I shouldn't have, Theia. Broke into your apartment. Watched you through your windows." I swallow, my gaze on hers. "I'm fucking obsessed with you, sunflower."

"I'm obsessed with you too."

It's cute she thinks that, but she doesn't know what obsession is. Not yet. She will.

"I'd stroke my cock like this while I watched you. You made him hurt so fucking bad. I jerked him raw thinking about all the shit I would do to you if you were mine. Couldn't help it," I mutter, a little afraid she's going to kick my ass. I wouldn't blame her. I know damn well that doing it crossed lines that shouldn't be crossed. I don't regret it.

"You watched me?"

I nod, not sure what she's thinking. If she's creeped out. If she's ready to run. I won't lie to her though. She was the light in the dark, the one place I found solace. I sought her out because I couldn't resist. And seeing her, watching her laugh with her friend or dance in her kitchen...I couldn't resist jerking my cock like a grade-A creep. Imagining being the reason for her smile, being the one she shook her ass for.

"I thought about you too," she says, so fucking sweetly cum spills from the head of my cock to coat my fingertips. "Every time I touched myself, I thought about you."

"Fuck," I growl, striding toward the bed. "Did you scream my name, Theia?"

"Yes," she whispers.

I groan, pissed I missed it. Pissed it took me so long to get my shit together. Pissed that she's had to get herself off for six months. Not anymore. When she comes now, it'll be my fingers, my tongue, my cock doing the work.

"Can I tie you up, sunflower?" I ask, leaving the choice up to her.

"Yes."

I lean down to kiss her. "You can say no anytime," I remind her.

"I know."

I quickly wrap my tie around her wrists and then bind it to the headboard, ensuring it's not tight enough to hurt her. She makes a beautiful sacrifice with her arms bound together over her head. The position pushes her tits together. I want to stick my dick between them.

"How does that feel?"

"Good," she moans. Already, she's breathing hard, her tits shuddering as she sucks air into her lungs. There isn't a hint of fear in her eyes though. Only excitement. Desire.

"If you need me to stop, you say stop, understand?" I ask.

"Yes," she says.

"Good girl." Content that she's comfortable and knows she's the one in control, I set to work, touching her like I've wanted to do for six fucking months. I run my hands all over her lush body, marveling at the way her soft body molds to my hands.

Heat engulfs me, flames leaving scorch marks on my self-control. I lean down over the bed, capturing one hard nipple in my mouth. Her little cry of ecstasy drives me higher. I toy with her, sucking and biting until her nipple is red with my marks. And then I move to the other, teasing her as mercilessly as she teased me. I already know once I get inside her, I won't be able to control myself. I want her as high as I can get her first.

My name rolls from her lips in an endless chant as I work my way down her body, lavishing her with attention. I nip and bite, leaving love bites all over her. Every single one makes my fucking cock throb and my balls ache.

She screams when I yank her legs apart and dive face first into her pussy. I don't give her time to think about it or prepare. I want her off guard and trembling on the edge, wondering what I'm gong to do to her next. How I'm going to touch her next, taste her next.

I roar when I get my first lick of her, what little restrain I have exploding into nothing. She's sweet peaches and juicy pussy...and so fucking *mine*.

If anyone else is in the building, I know they hear me eating her. I'm relentless, snarling against her pussy, rubbing my face in it, lapping at her clit like a fucking dog. I spear my tongue into her, thrusting it inside her little fuckhole in ruthless strikes, trying to get deeper, to taste that tart cherry on my tongue.

The headboard rattles as she yanks at the tie, sobbing, babbling.

I pry her cheeks apart, fucking that little hole with my tongue too. Back and forth until her entire body locks up, a shrill scream ripping through the room. It annihilates the shadows clinging to the corners, lighting them up with holy fire.

"Again," I snarl, incapable of stopping what I'm doing to her. She tastes too fucking good. *Looks* too fucking good. Sounds too good. Goddamn, had I known she'd go this wild for me, honor wouldn't have been enough to keep me from claiming her six months ago. Nothing would have.

She thrashes and wails, riding my face from beneath. I replace my tongue in her ass with my thumb, gently pressing it against the tight ring of muscle before working it inside her. I shouldn't be doing it, but that won't stop me. Every time I see this ass in her cute little skirts, I think about being balls deep in it.

"Relax, sunflower," I growl when she tenses. "This is mine to play with how I want."

"Masen, oh my god."

I suck on her clit, riding my tongue over the hood. Her body goes pliant beneath me. My thumb slips into her ass. I work it in and out of that tight little hole slowly, letting her get used to it. It doesn't take long until she's whining my name.

"Masen. Masen, I...I..."

I don't need her to say it to know what she needs. I give it to her without hesitation, burying my face in her pussy and fucking her ass with my thumb at the same time. I'm ruthless, brutally dragging her toward a second orgasm and then a third.

Her entire body bows off the bed before crashing back down. I rear up over her, yanking her legs up around my hips. My dick lands against her pussy. I lean down, kissing her hard and deep. I'm not sure which one of us is more wrecked. I haven't even gotten inside her and I'm shaking.

"You like being my little plaything, Theia?" I ask, lining myself up at her entrance.

"Masen," she whimpers.

"Answer me, sunflower."

"Yes!" she cries. "I love it!"

"Yeah, you do. This body is mine. I'll do what I want to it, when I want."

"Yes," she agrees, undulating beneath me.

"If you don't want my kids, you better tell me now. Otherwise, I'm taking you bare and I'm not stopping until you're pregnant." I know she wants kids. I plan to give her as many as she wants. She'll make a hell of a mother.

"Yes," she whispers, chasing my lips with hers.

"I love you."

"Masen!" she screams as I slam myself inside of her, ripping through her hymen.

The sound of her pain shreds my heart, ripping through my insides like claws. Hurting her hurts like hell. She should only ever feel pleasure in this bed. From now on, that's all my body will ever give her.

"Kiss me, sunflower," I whisper against her lips, nudging her nose with mine. "Let me take the pain away again."

Her kiss is tentative at first, her mind tangled up in the pain. I pour my soul into her, stealing her breath and the pain from her, making it my own. I can take it. For her, I will take it. We kiss for a long time, getting lost in one another. She relaxes slowly, her muscles unlocking one by one.

I revel in the tight clasp of her body around mine, in the heat of her cunt branding my cock, in the softness of her curves cradling mine. I don't move, not an inch.

The need to fuck and claim churns through me, growing in intensity, demanding I ride her hard. Only when she's pliant in my arms do I give in to the urge.

I rock my hips slowly, giving her time to adjust.

She moans, her mouth popping open.

"Fuck, I love this pussy," I groan, leaning back to watch myself fuck her. Droplets of blood smear with her cream, coating my cock. It's the sexiest fucking thing I've ever seen.

"Masen," she moans, rocking her hips as if to urge me on.

I rear back and then push forward, impaling her on my cock. Harder and then faster. She feels so fucking good. There's no way I'm going to survive this. I kiss her again and then again, getting lost in the driving rhythm, in her sweet pleas for more. My balls meet her ass in loud claps of sound. The headboard taps against the wall.

The rest of the world disappears. I fuck her harder. Deeper. Pounding into her again and then again, unable to stop myself. I'm a madman, a lion set loose on a lamb. I fuck her from one orgasm to the next, demanding another and then another. Every time that cunt locks down on my dick, I roar in triumph.

It's too much. I know it is. Yet I don't stop. I *can't* stop. Fuck lust consumes me, the need to fuck my way into her soul driving me. She fights against her bonds, wailing my name, trying to get her hands on me as another orgasm takes her.

"Please," she gasps. "Please."

"Take it, Theia," I demand.

"I can't. I can't," she sobs.

"You can." I slow my pace to nuzzle my face into her sweaty throat. "Give me one more, sunflower. You can take it."

"Masen," she whimpers.

"I'll catch you," I promise. I'll always catch her.

"One m-more," she sobs.

I turn my head, pressing a kiss to her lips. I take her slow this time, whispering praises in her ear, kissing all over her throat, worshipping her like the goddess she is. We move together, writhe together. Until her cunt locks down on my cock, her teeth on my shoulder.

I roar my release into the room, her name on my lips. Cum shoots up my shaft, pouring into her so hard it hurts. Christ, it hurts. Everything but her disappears, our bodies locked together in a dance of agony, a song of bliss, one so perfect nothing else matters. I know it never will again.

"It's midnight," I whisper, running my hands through her hair. We haven't moved in an hour. We haven't said much either. We're just here in this moment. Together. I've never felt peace like this, never felt completion like this.

"Happy New Year, Masen." She turns her head, placing a kiss on my chest.

"Happy New Year, sunflower."

She settles back down on my chest, running her fingers up and down my side. "Can I ask..." She bites her lip and lifts her head, looking up at me through her lashes. "What happened?"

"You can ask."

"I know you can't tell me." Sadness sweeps through her expression as she leans over me. Her lips touch the top of my scar, right over my ribcage. "I'm sorry for what you went through."

Ah, God. She's killing me and doesn't even know it.

"Militia," I growl, not giving a damn if I am breaking about nine laws by telling her. I have no secrets from her. I'll tell her anything she wants to know. "They swept through a village and scooped up a bunch of boys. The militias like to use them as soldiers. The TLPF got their hands on them and were trying to use them to force Sudan into a conflict the region can't afford. We were sent in on a covert operation to rescue them."

"Oh." She lifts her gaze to mine. "Did you?"

She reads the truth in my eyes, her face falling.

"Oh, Masen," she whispers, tears filling her eyes.

"We were ambushed," I rasp. "The TLPF set us up, pointed a militia right at us. Most of them were just fucking kids themselves, but they hit us with everything they had. We were outnumbered and outgunned, with twenty-three little boys to protect. We lost all but two of my teammates and six of the boys. They dragged me out of there. If a couple of Sudanese farmers hadn't stumbled across us, I wouldn't have made it out."

A tear slips down her cheek. I catch it on my fingertip, and then sweep my hand across the plane of her cheek.

"Come here, sunflower." I gently drag her up my chest and into my arms, holding her tight. "Don't cry for me, Theia. It's over and done with now."

"I'll cry for you if I want to, Masen Starks," she huffs, her voice thick with her tears. Even so, the comment makes me smile.

For the first time, talking about what happened doesn't have memories threatening to intrude. It's as if they know they hold no sway here, not when she's in my arms. I'm bulletproof in this moment, bigger than my past and the fucked up shit I went through. *She* makes me bulletproof.

"You help," I murmur, rubbing her back. "More than you know. When I got here, I didn't care if I lived or not. Every fucking night, I relived it. I watched us fail those kids over and over. The day I met you, I knew I had to find a way to survive it."

"What changed your mind?"

"Knowing you lost your dad," I say. "You were the sweetest little angel with no one watching out for you, no one to protect you. I had to survive it to take over where he left off."

"Masen," she whispers.

I roll to the right, pulling her over with me. She lands on her back beneath me, staring up at me with those bright eyes that see clean through to my soul. They're watery, but still so fucking beautiful.

"I want to take you somewhere tomorrow."

"Where?"

"To show you something."

"Is it your penis?" she asks, narrowing her eyes in suspicion.

I shake my head, chuckling. "No, smart ass. It's not my dick."

"Oh." She pouts for a minute and then smiles. "I guess I'll go with you then."

"Were you going to say no if it was my dick?"

"I mean...I did just see it." She shrugs, pure mischief in her eyes.

I reach for her, covering her body with my own as her laughter rings out around us.

CHAPTER NINE
Theia

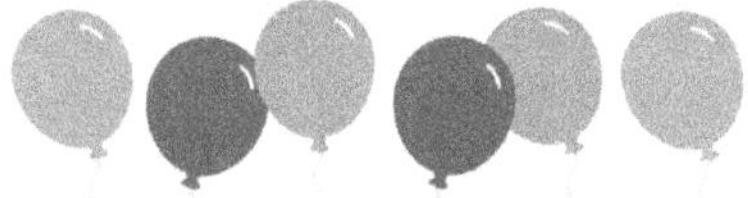

"**W**here are we going?" I ask Masen for the hundredth time since he took me by my place to change an hour ago. We're in the foothills of the Laguna Mountains, slowly climbing higher. The winter sun shines brightly overhead and there isn't a cloud in sight. It's a perfect start to the new year, a better start than I could have ever dreamed of.

"You'll see."

I groan loudly. He won't give me even a hint of where we're going.

"Don't make me make you play with yourself until we get there, sunflower," he growls, cutting his eyes in my direction. His expression is hot, pure wickedness in those blue eyes. "You know how much I like listening to you make that cunt sloppy for me."

"Masen!" I cry, placing my hands over my red face. He's had his tongue in places it probably isn't supposed to be, but the things he says.... Lord above, he's wicked.

His deep chuckle sends a frisson of heat through me.

He reaches for my hands, tugging them away from my face. "Don't hide from me, Theia. We have no secrets," he murmurs, bringing one hand up to his lips to kiss the back of it. "Besides, we both know how I'm not the only one who likes it."

"Masen," I groan, making him laugh again.

He places my hand on his thigh and then reaches for the radio to turn it up. Classic rock spills into the truck. I glance out the window, watching the trees pass us by, listening to him hum along to the radio. He's so damn happy.

Hearing what he went through broke my heart into tiny picccs last night. I knew it was bad, but I never imagined it was so awful. Kids killing kids for a cause they don't even understand. Him, forced to watch it happen, unable to stop it. He is the strongest person I know, hands down. I know him and I know his heart. I know how deeply losing those boys cut. But he's still here. He's still fighting. I'll be thanking God for that every day for the rest of my life.

When the burden gets too heavy for him to carry, I'll help him shoulder it. Whatever he needs, I'll do. He deserves to know every single day that he isn't fighting alone. And he *isn't* fighting alone. I may not be a soldier or a sailor. But I'll be a warrior for him. I'll be *his* soldier.

The truck slows.

Masen pulls off the road, the tires crunching over gravel. The truck rises and then falls as it climbs over deep potholes in the narrow gravel lane. Trees press in on us from every side, casting the cab into shadows.

Before I can ask any questions, the road widens. We drive out into a clearing a moment later. My breath catches in my throat when I see the view.

"Oh, Masen," I whisper, staring in awe at the mountains rising on the far side of the clearing. And then I notice the log cabin off to the left. It's clearly under construction, but the outer walls are up and so is the roof. A wraparound porch surrounds the front, with a smaller balcony leading off of the second story.

Masen pulls up in front of the cabin and parks.

"Where are we?" I ask.

He winks at me and then kills the engine, not speaking.

"Masen!" I cry when he climbs out. I swear, he drives me crazy! He never answers questions when I ask them. He always makes me wait, and then gives me answers at the most unexpected times. I think he does it intentionally to torture me.

"Come on, sunflower," he says, popping my door open.

"You're annoying and I'm going to strangle you," I inform him as he helps me out of the truck.

"Yeah?" Humor dances in his eyes and across his handsome face. He puts me on my feet, wrapping his hand around my throat. "You're the one who likes having a hand around your throat, Theia."

"Do not," I lie.

"Liar."

I huff, rolling my eyes at him.

He chuckles, lacing our fingers together. We walk in silence toward the cabin. He stops me with a hand on my shoulder at the front door and then sweeps me up into his arms.

"What are you doing?" I ask, amused.

"There are loose nails," he says. "Don't want you to step on one."

My heart flutters. I swear, he's a whole dichotomy. Sometimes, he's so damn sweet he makes my teeth ache. Other times, like last night, he's a dark prince, ruthless and commanding. I love both sides of him so much.

He carries me inside. The house isn't far along yet. The walls are still exposed wood. Electrical lines and pipes run here and there throughout. But even half finished, it's beautiful. When it's complete, it'll be gorgeous. It's not overwhelmingly large, but big enough for a family. A large fireplace takes up half of one wall. Empty windowpanes looking out over the mountains and the valley below dominate the back wall.

"Where are we, Masen?"

"Three months ago, I tried to convince myself that I had to leave you," he murmurs, carrying me deeper into the room. "I knew I didn't deserve you, didn't think I ever could deserve you. I still don't think I ever will."

"I'm the one who doesn't deserve you," I say, cupping his cheek.

He turns his head, pressing a kiss to my palm. "Before you even shed a tear that day, I knew I couldn't follow through, Theia. I couldn't leave you. When you left the daycare that day, I knew I had to get my shit together. I had to find a way to deserve you. I went to see a realtor."

"Masen, are you saying...?"

"I grew up in foster care. I never had a home until I met you. I know you grew up moving from base to base. You never had a home either," he says and then swallows hard. "I want this to be your home."

"Masen," I whisper.

"I'm building it for you, sunflower. That's why it took me so goddamn long to make a move. I wanted to have it finished before I made you mine, but Killian is a slick motherfucker."

"I was never going anywhere with Marco," I say.

"I know. Killian decided to meddle."

"I'm glad he did."

"Me too." His lips curve into a ghost of a smile. "You deserve more than a dorm room, and I wanted you to have that. I wanted to be a man worthy of you. And I needed time to get my head on straight, to work through my shit. But I don't regret claiming you early, sunflower."

"Are you asking me to move in here with you?" I ask, teasing him.

"No." He leans down, setting me carefully on a crate in the middle of the room. Once I'm steady, he kneels in front of me, reaching into his pocket. His eyes lock with mine. "I'm not asking you to live here with me, Theia. I'm asking you to marry me."

"Masen," I gasp, staring in shock at the gorgeous platinum and solitary ring between his fingers.

"You're mine, sunflower. You have been for six months. I couldn't love you then like you deserved. But I'll spend the rest of my life making it up to you," he whispers, his eyes locked on mine. "You're my soul. I don't deserve you, but no one else does either. No one will ever worship you like I do, Theia. Let me prove it."

"Yes," I sob, frantically nodding my head. "Yes, I'll marry you."

"Fuck." Emotion pulses in his eyes, moisture turning them bright. He grabs my hand, sliding the ring onto my finger. As soon as he has it in place, I launch myself off the crate and into his arms, wrapping around him like a Koala. His strong arms surround me, pulling me up against his chest.

"I love you so much," I cry, sobbing into his throat.

"I know you do, sunflower. I feel it every time you look at me." He crooks a finger under my chin, tipping my head back until our eyes connect. His overflow with joy. With peace. "I've loved you every second, every minute, every day since I met you. I always will, sunflower. *Always.*"

His promise echoes in my soul, tumbling every piece of it into his hands. I press my lips to his, sealing his promise with a kiss. His lips move with mine, giving me the first beautiful taste of forever.

EPILOGUE
Masen

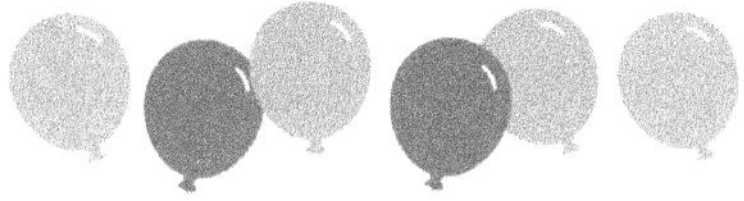

Five Years Later

"Hands flat on the desk," I growl, crowding Theia up against the antique wood. "Ass in the air."

"Masen," she moans, writhing when I reach around her to pinch her nipples. She does what I say though, sliding her hands out flat on the desk and lifting her ass high into the air for me.

I make her wait for what she wants, teasing her like she's always doing to me. My wife is a kinky little thing. She loves slipping her hand into my pants at every available opportunity or brushing that round ass up against me. It doesn't matter where we are, if she can find a way to torture me without anyone seeing, she'll do it. She gets off on making me sweat. I think she gets off on the risk of getting caught too. She'll never admit that one though.

I've fucked her every which way I can fuck her. I've had my cock in one hole and a vibrator in the other. I've tied her down and tied her up. Taken her with my hand around her throat while she was pinned to the bed. I've done every filthy thing in the book to her. She's begged for them, screamed for them. And still, she's the sweetest little sunflower I've ever met.

I thought I'd soil her. I was wrong. After five years of my filth, she still shines as bright as ever. I don't worry about soiling her anymore. She's a fucking warrior for good, the best defense this world has against true darkness. I should know. She's been keeping mine at bay for five years.

"Please," she groans, her chest falling toward the top of my desk as her arms lose power.

I line up with her soaked pussy and yank her onto me.

We cry out in unison as her slick heat surrounds my length. I stay still for a split second, giving her a chance to take a breath. As soon as she does, I wrap her ponytail around my fist and pound into her, fucking her hard and fast. It's what she wants. It's why she's been fucking with me since she popped into my office an hour ago, waving that round ass in my face, arching her back to show me her tits.

My little sunflower needs to come. She's four months pregnant and horny as hell.

"Is this what you wanted, sunflower?" I ask, craning her head back. "You've been fucking with me all throughout lunch, trying to get yourself bent over and fucked."

"Yes," she moans without hesitation. "Need you."

I cover her mouth with mine, my heart pulsing with emotion. She never holds anything back from me. I'm the same with her. There are no secrets between us, nothing we can't discuss or reveal. Whatever she wants, all she has to do is ask and it's hers. She likes when I take what I want though. She complains that I'm bossy, but we both know she fucking loves every minute of it. She certainly does everything in her power to rile me up.

I kiss her while I fuck her, pounding into that tight cunt like it's mine to wreck. It is. No one else will ever touch it. It's been five years, and I'm as possessive of this little sunflower as ever. She's the center of my world, the reason I exist. The way she loves me... God, there's nothing like it. I feel the force of her love, every minute of the day.

She reminds me of it every night when she's lying in my arms, her head on my chest. And in the mornings when she slips into my arms in the kitchen and lets me hold her.

And a thousand times in between. Those words flow from her lips like honey, spoken without reservation.

I remind her too. Every fucking chance I get. It'll never be enough to satisfy me. She's dragged me back from the edge more times than I can count over the last five years, brought me back to life again and again. Whenever the past creeps up, she's there, guarding my back like a warrior. When the nightmares hit, she's there, holding me through them. She isn't my weakness. She's my strength. My purpose. I am because she is.

I'll spend the rest of my life loving her. It still won't be enough. That's all right though. Whatever comes after this life, I'll find her there. I'll love her there. My soul is hers, not just now but always.

"Come then, sunflower," I demand, pumping my hips so I hit her g-spot with every thrust. "Cream on my cock like a good girl." I lick into her mouth, swallowing her moan as she writhes on my cock. When I'm not in her, the filthy things I say to her make her blush. But when she's on my cock, she can't get enough of my mouth.

Her pussy clamps down on my cock, her cream soaking me as she ignites. I thrust deep, growling her name as she unravels around me, pulling me over the edge with her. Her sweet cries ring out around us, sending me straight to heaven.

She shakes and trembles and then falls still, so fucking beautiful. So fucking sweet.

"Sunflower," I whisper, spinning her around. My mouth comes down on hers, my arms surrounding her, pulling her up against my chest. I kiss her gently, reverently. "I love you."

"I love you," she whispers back, pliant in my arms.

I hold her close, reveling in this peaceful moment with her. Sex with her is out of this world. But the moments right after, when she's purring in my arms...those are my favorite. With three boys under the age of four, I cherish every quiet moment I get with her. Lord knows, they do not make getting her alone easy. They're as obsessed with their mama as I am.

I can't even blame them for it. She's an incredible mom. Our boys love nothing more than to be near her. I love how protective they are of her. I know they'll be just as protective of their little sister when she gets here in a few months. I certainly will. If she's even half as sweet as my sunflower, I'm going to lose my fucking mind trying to keep her safe. Thank God she has three older brothers to help me do it.

Our boys may be a handful, but I wouldn't trade them for a fucking thing. My wife and kids are my life. I fought for this country, killed for it. I wouldn't hesitate to do the same for my family. They're mine to protect, mine to guard. Nothing touches them, nothing hurts them. I won't allow it.

"I should get back to the daycare," Theia says. "Sam needs to leave early."

"You'll be on your own this afternoon?" I ask, frowning. I worry about her, especially when she's pregnant. It's my job to worry about her. She finished her degree two years ago and now runs the daycare and a number of programs here for parents returning from warzones. Her favorite place is still in the daycare with the kids though. She loves them so much.

"No. Liberty is going to come help out," she assures me, tipping her head back to smile at me. Her expression is soft and full of love. "I'll be fine, Masen."

I tip my head down to hers, nibbling on her lips. "I like worrying about you."

"I know," she says, rolling her eyes.

I narrow mine on her. "Did I not give you enough to satisfy you, sunflower? Because you're itching for a spanking rolling those eyes at me."

"Bossy."

I shake my head, chuckling when I see the mischief in her eyes. That's exactly what she's after. I kiss her hard on the mouth and then swat her ass. "Let's get you put back together so you can get back to work, baby girl."

"Fine," she says, pouting at me.

I clean her up carefully and then help her get her clothes on. She glares at me when she has to pull her ponytail down and redo it. I just shrug, not in the least contrite. She loves when I get my hands in her hair and we both know it.

Once I've got my dick tucked back in my pants and she's put back together, I pull her into my arms for another kiss. "When the boys go down tonight, I have something for you," I murmur against her lips.

"A spanking isn't a present, Masen," she says, laughing against my lips.

"The spanking isn't the present. It's the punishment for that smart ass mouth."

She moans, making me smile.

"Damn," I breathe, stopping in the bedroom doorway to stare at Theia. She's in front of the full-length mirror, wearing nothing but her panties as she runs her hands over her bump, her expression soft. Some women are miserable when they're pregnant. Not Theia. The entire process is magical to her. She loves carrying my babies.

I think she'd stay pregnant all the time if she could. But we've both decided Calandria will be our last. Or so we say. I have a feeling Theia will be talking me into another one as soon as Calandria is out of diapers. I have a feeling it won't take much to convince me to get her pregnant again.

There's nothing more beautiful in this world than my wife when she's carrying my babies.

"Your daughter decided to get up when the boys went down," she says, smiling at me in the mirror. "She's having a party in there."

I step into the room, pushing the door closed behind me. I just checked on the boys. All three are passed out cold. They won't move until morning. Thank God. I've got plans for their mama tonight.

I prowl across the room toward her, pressing up against her from behind to wrap my arms around her. I rest my head on her shoulder, kissing her neck. She moans and tilts it to the side, giving me more room.

"Hi, sweet girl," I croon to our daughter, splaying my hand wide across Theia's belly. "I know you're a night owl, but I'm going to need you to settle down in there so I can do dirty things to your mommy."

"Masen," Theia says, her body shaking with laughter. "You can't tell our baby you're going to do dirty things to me."

"She's the size of a banana, sunflower," I murmur, nuzzling her neck. "She doesn't know what the fuck I'm saying. All she hears are vibrations."

"She isn't the only banana," she sasses, pressing her ass into me.

"I'll let you choke on mine later," I mutter, reaching into my pocket. "But first, do you know what today is?"

"Thursday."

"Smart ass."

She grins at me.

"Five years ago today, I saw the sweetest little sunflower and my life changed."

"You remember the date we met?" she whispers, awe in her eyes.

"How could I forget? Hold out your hand."

She obediently holds it out for me, allowing me to drop her present into her palm.

"Oh," she whispers as soon as her gaze drops to the golden sunflower on a thin gold chain. She strokes a fingertip across the petals of the flower, her expression soft. "It's so beautiful."

"Open it."

She glances over her shoulder at me and then down at the necklace. It only takes her a couple of seconds to find the hidden catch. The sunflower splits in two, revealing the message tucked carefully behind the petals.

You are my light, sunflower.

"Masen," she breathes.

"It's true," I say, turning her in my arms. "I call you my sunflower because you're a warrior, Theia. You stand tall and reach toward the light no matter what. You never falter. You pull that light down to you and radiate it into the world. With you in my arms, the dark doesn't stand a chance, baby girl. It never did."

She sobs my name, flinging her arms around my neck.

I pull her up against me, breathing her in.

"Thank you for bringing me back to life," I whisper in her hair. "Thank you for loving me."

She sobs again, practically climbing my body. I boost her up into my arms, holding her tight as she cries into my throat, clinging like she's never going to let me go.

"You're my light too, Masen," she says through her tears. "I grow toward you."

"Jesus," I whisper, pressing my face into her hair. This woman... God, this woman. Even after five years, she finds new ways to make me fall for her. She takes me to new heights, propelling me into entirely new levels of heaven.

I'll always have PTSD, but I'm not worried about sinking into hell anymore. How could I be when I've got her here, lighting up the dark like the sun?

"I love you, sunflower," I whisper, carrying her toward the bed, desperate to make love to her again. To be connected to her again in a way that's deeper than physical, more than merely fucking. When I'm in her, I'm whole. And so is she.

"I love you," she whispers, her lips seeking mine. "Every second. Every minute. Every day."

"Always," I promise.

Author's Note

If you enjoyed *Angel Kisses*, please consider leaving a review! I appreciate them so much!

Liberty and Killian's story, Possessing Liberty, is available in the Claimed series!

Possessing Liberty

<u>Excerpt</u>

"**Y**ou're late," I growl. My dick is so hard it's painful. I can't think through the wall of lust pounding through me in relentless waves. The things I'm going to teach this girl. Jesus Christ, I should be ashamed of the filthy, kinky shit I'm going to do to her. I'm not. The coil of anticipation in my stomach winds tighter, cinching my balls up tight.

"It's 7:45," she says, her honey-eyes flashing with annoyance. "You said be here at eight."

Damn. It feels later.

"Come with me," I mutter, turning on my heel. I take a deep breath, trying to get myself under control again. It's impossible. I smell her like she's been all over me. She smells like coconut and sugar, reminding me of the pies our nanny used to make for us. I have a feeling she's going to taste even better than they did.

Her heels click against the floor as she follows behind me. She doesn't speak to me, though I hear her muttering beneath her breath. She's probably calling me a jackass. I don't know how to be soft and sweet like she deserves. It doesn't come natural to me, but I want to try though.

I stop outside the office we're sharing and hold the door open for her.

Her body brushes against mine when she ducks through. I fight back the hungry growl threatening to erupt. Slow. I need to take it slow with her. Give her time to trust me. And then I can fuck her until she's pleading for mercy.

She freezes right over the threshold, going stock still. "We're sharing an office?"

"Don't have an extra one," I lie.

"You didn't say we'd be sharing an office."

"Forgot," I lie again, ducking in behind her. I didn't forget and we don't have to share an office, but we're going to anyway. I want her where I can see her. She's far prettier than any view I've had lately. There is beauty in nature, but that beauty doesn't show up often in the kind of places I've spent the last fifteen years inhabiting.

Her irritation vanishes when she notices the flowers on her desk. She turns to face me, her expression soft. "You got me flowers?"

"And a blanket," I mutter. "I like it cold."

"Thank you," she whispers.

We stare at each other for a long, silent moment before I move toward her, slipping the purse off her shoulder to drop it on her desk. I tip her face up toward me so I can see her clearly. Her eyes are dark beneath even though she tried to hide the shadows with makeup.

"You're tired."

"I didn't sleep well."

"You don't like me."

She blinks at me, caught off guard. "I don't know you enough to dislike you," she says, being honest with me. "You make me nervous."

"Why?"

"You're...different than anyone I know." Her cheeks heat, her gaze slipping away from mine before it comes right back like she can't help herself.

"Different how?"

She shrugs, looking away again. Interesting. She can't face me when she's lying. I file that information away for later.

"Different how?"

"The way you look at me," she says, taking a breath and meeting my gaze again. She holds it, refusing to look away this time. "No one ever looks at me like you do."

"That's because I see you." I hesitate for a brief moment, and then decide to go for broke. I want her to know where this thing between us is headed. She wants me too. Even if she never admits it, I know she wouldn't be here right now if she wasn't interested. "You had my dick hard before you ever opened your mouth."

A pretty blush blooms on her cheeks. She doesn't tell me to go to hell or slap me, so I take that as a good sign.

"You're not so bad yourself," she finally says, looking at me from beneath those long, sooty lashes. "You look like a warrior." She laughs a little. "I guess that's fitting, huh?"

"You like looking at me?"

She rolls her eyes. "I'm sure women are always hitting on you."

"You'd be wrong," I mutter.

She blinks at me, clearly surprised. Which is just fucking cute. The fact that she's attracted to me makes me feel ten feet tall and bullet proof.

"I haven't dated in years."

"Oh." She frowns, her brow crinkling. "Why not?"

"Until six months ago, I was in the desert. Since then? No one has caught my attention." I meet her gaze, holding it. "Not until yesterday."

She blushes again, making my cock leak.

"What about you?"

"I don't date either."

"Not yet you don't," I mutter, releasing her before I do something she'll regret and kiss her. "That'll be changing."

Possessing Liberty is now available!

DIRTY BOY

Can this dirty boy convince his curvy girl that love is worth any risk?

Dante

Behind my back, people call me rude.

To my face, they call me a star.

I never cared what anyone had to say.

All that mattered to me was football and my family.

The minute I saw Ella Morgan, everything changed.

Now all I think about is that sweet smile.

She thinks we're just a summer fling. She's wrong.

There's nothing temporary about the way she makes me feel.

One way or another, this curvy little goddess will be mine.

Even if I have to play dirty to win her.

Ella

Last week, I destroyed my drug-dealing father's supply and skipped town.

All I want to do is lay low until school starts.

Except Dante Duncan refuses to leave me alone.

He's the biggest, bossiest football star I've ever seen.

He says we're meant to be.

I'm starting to believe he might be right.

But I don't need the kind of attention he draws.

I promised myself I wouldn't fall for him.

Except I'm pretty sure it's already too late.

How am I supposed to say goodbye at the end of the summer?

If you enjoy steamy sweet romance, summer love, and bossy men who know exactly what they want, you'll love Dante and Ella's dirty hot story!

Dirty Boy is available on all retailers!

Instalove Book Club

The Instalove Book Club is now in session!

Get the inside scoop from your favorite instalove authors, meet new authors to love, and snag freebies and bonus content from featured authors every month. The Instalove Book Club newsletter goes out once per week!

Join now to get your hands on bonus scenes and brand-new, exclusive content from our first six featured authors.

Join the Club: http://instalovebookclub.com

FOLLOW NICHOLE

Sign-up for the mailing list to stay up to date on all new releases and for exclusive ARC giveaways from Nichole Rose.

Want to connect with Nichole and other readers?

Join Nichole Rose's Book Beauties on Facebook!

facebook.com/AuthorNicholeRose/

instagram.com/AuthorNicholeRose

twitter.com/AuthNicholeRose

bookbub.com/authors/nichole-rose

tiktok.com/@authornicholerose

More by Nichole Rose

<u>Her Alpha Series</u>

Her Alpha Daddy Next Door

Her Alpha Boss Undercover

Her Alpha's Secret Baby

Her Alpha Protector

Her Date with an Alpha

Her Alpha: The Complete Series

<u>Her Bride Series</u>

His Future Bride

His Stolen Bride

His Secret Bride

His Curvy Bride

His Captive Bride

His Blushing Bride

His Bride: The Complete Series

Claimed Series

Possessing Liberty

Teaching Rowan

Claiming Caroline

Kissing Kennedy

Claimed: The Complete Series

Love on the Clock Series

Adore You

Hold You

Keep You

Protect You

Love on the Clock: The Complete Series

The Billionaires' Club

The Billionaire's Big Bold Weakness

The Billionaire's Big Bold Wish

The Billionaire's Big Bold Woman

The Billionaire's Big Bold Wonder

<u>Playing for Keeps</u>

Cutie Pie

Ice Breaker

Ice Prince

Ice Giant (coming soon)

<u>The Second Generation</u>

A Blushing Bride for Christmas

Come Undone (currently in Love Always Wins anthology)

<u>Silver Spoon MC</u>

The Surgeon

The Heir

The Lawyer

The Prodigy (coming soon)

The Bodyguard (coming soon)

<u>Echoes of Forever</u>

His Christmas Miracle

Taken by the Hitman

Wicked Saint

The Ruined Trilogy

Physical Science

Wrecked

Destination Romance

Romancing the Cowboy

Beach House Beauty

Standalone Titles

A Touch of Summer

Black Velvet

His Secret Obsession

Dirty Boy

Naughty Little Elf

Devil's Deceit

Wearing Their Pearls (coming soon)

Easy on Me

Easy Ride

Easy Surrender

One Night with You

Falling Hard

Model Behavior

Learning Curve

Angel Kisses

writing with Loni Ree as Loni Nichole

Dillon's Heart (coming soon)

Razor's Flame (coming soon)

Ryker's Reward (coming soon)

Zane's Rebel (coming soon)

About Nichole Rose

Nichole Rose is a short romance author on the west coast. Her books feature headstrong, sassy women and the alpha males who consume them. From grumpy detectives to country boys with attitude to instalove and over-the-top declarations, nothing is off-limits.

Nichole is sure to have a steamy, sweet story just right for everyone. She fully believes the world is ugly enough without trying to fit falling in love into a one-size-fits-all box. When not writing, Nichole enjoys fine wine, cute shoes, and everything supernatural. She is happily married to the love of her life and is a proud mama to the world's most ridiculous fur-babies.

You can learn more about Nichole and her books at her website .

facebook.com/AuthorNicholeRose/

instagram.com/AuthorNicholeRose

twitter.com/AuthNicholeRose

bookbub.com/authors/nichole-rose

tiktok.com/@authornicholerose